Monica Ferris's other Needlecraft Mysteries:

UNRAVELED SLEEVE

"A comfortable fit for mystery readers who want to spend an enjoyable time with interesting characters."
— *St. Paul (MN) Pioneer Press*

A STITCH IN TIME

"A fun read that baffles the reader with mystery and delights with . . . romance." — *Romantic Times*

FRAMED IN LACE

"An enjoyable, classy tale. Betsy is everyone's favorite grandma, who proves life begins after fifty . . . Engaging . . . A fun-to-read story." — *Midwest Book Review*

CREWEL WORLD

"Filled with great small-town characters . . . A great time."
— *Rendezvous*

"Fans of Margaret Yorke will relate to Betsy's growth and eventual maturity . . . You need not be a needlecrafter to enjoy this delightful series debut." — *Mystery Time*

A
MURDEROUS
YARN

Monica Ferris

BERKLEY PRIME CRIME, NEW YORK

THE BERKLEY PUBLISHING GROUP
Published by the Penguin Group
Penguin Group (USA) Inc.
375 Hudson Street, New York, New York 10014, USA
Penguin Group (Canada), 90 Eglinton Avenue East, Suite 700, Toronto, Ontario M4P 2Y3, Canada
(a division of Pearson Penguin Canada Inc.)
Penguin Books Ltd., 80 Strand, London WC2R 0RL, England
Penguin Group Ireland, 25 St. Stephen's Green, Dublin 2, Ireland (a division of Penguin Books Ltd.)
Penguin Group (Australia), 250 Camberwell Road, Camberwell, Victoria 3124, Australia
(a division of Pearson Australia Group Pty. Ltd.)
Penguin Books India Pvt. Ltd., 11 Community Centre, Panchsheel Park, New Delhi—110 017, India
Penguin Group (NZ), Cnr. Airborne and Rosedale Roads, Albany, Auckland 1310, New Zealand
(a division of Pearson New Zealand Ltd.)
Penguin Books (South Africa) (Pty.) Ltd., 24 Sturdee Avenue, Rosebank, Johannesburg 2196,
South Africa

Penguin Books Ltd., Registered Offices: 80 Strand, London WC2R 0RL, England

This is a work of fiction. Names, characters, places, and incidents either are the product of the author's imagination or are used fictitiously, and any resemblance to actual persons, living or dead, business establishments, events, or locales is entirely coincidental. The publisher does not have any control over and does not assume any responsibility for author or third-party websites or their content.

A MURDEROUS YARN

A Berkley Prime Crime Book / published by arrangement with the author

PRINTING HISTORY
Berkley Prime Crime mass-market edition / March 2002

Copyright © 2002 by Mary Monica Kuhfeld.
Cover art by Mary Anne Lasher.

ISBN: 0-425-18403-X

BERKLEY ® PRIME CRIME
Berkley Prime Crime Books are published by The Berkley Publishing Group,
a division of Penguin Group (USA) Inc.,
375 Hudson Street, New York, New York 10014.
The name BERKLEY PRIME CRIME and the BERKLEY PRIME CRIME design
are trademarks belonging to Penguin Group (USA) Inc.

PRINTED IN THE UNITED STATES OF AMERICA

18 17 16 15 14 13 12 11 10 9

Acknowledgments

There really is an Antique Car Run from New London to New Brighton in Minnesota every summer, except it's held in August, not June. The members of the club, especially Jim and Dorothy Vergin and Ed Walhof, were incredibly helpful to me, patient with my ignorance, generous with information—even letting me ride in their cars. So if there's an error in this novel, it's my own fault for not listening more carefully. I would also like to thank Gene Grengs for letting me see how to start a Stanley Steamer, Pat Farrel out in Washington State for telling me how to use a Stanley to run down an SUV, and Fred Abbott out in Washington State for letting me "borrow" his magnificent 1912 Renault Sport Touring Car.

The shops Stitchville USA and Needlework Unlimited helped me keep on track with the details of Betsy's Crewel World, and the Internet news group RCTN again proved reliable when I had questions or problems or needed a good idea.

1

Spring came early to Excelsior that year. Everyone remarked that there had been no hard freezes since the fifth of March. The ice on Lake Minnetonka was rotten and great puddles gleamed like quicksilver on it. It was not yet St. Patrick's Day but the robins were back, mourning doves were sobbing, and daffodils budded in south-facing flower beds. Only yesterday, Betsy had been delighted to find a great wash of purple crocuses pushing through the flat layers of dead leaves on the steep, tree-strewn slope behind her apartment building.

She had noticed the rich purple color while taking out the trash. It had been the one good thing about the task. On that same trip, her vision downward blocked by boxes and black plastic bags, she had nearly fallen into one of the yawning potholes that menaced traffic in her small parking lot. And she'd had to put everything down while she struggled with the Dumpster's creaking lid, so rusted around the hinges it resisted being lifted.

How wonderful it would be, she had thought, to bring the trash out to the front sidewalk on Wednesdays for someone else to pick up and carry away. Even better, to dig up the crumbled blacktop parking lot, put in some topsoil, and plant tulips and bleeding hearts and old-fashioned varieties of roses, the kind whose scent lay heavy on the air in summer. And at the back, a row of benches under trellises covered alternately with honeysuckle and morning glories, to draw butterflies and hummingbirds. She'd stood beside the homely Dumpster for a minute, inhaling imaginary sweet-smelling air.

But her tenants' leases promised each a parking space and a container to put their refuse in any day of the week. She had been dismayed to discover how expensive it was to rent the Dumpster, and to have it emptied weekly. And by the estimate for resurfacing the parking lot. Being a landlord wasn't solely about collecting rents.

Now, the next morning, she sighed over her abysmal willingness to leap into things without first learning the consequences. She should have let Joe keep this moldy old building with its leaky roof, potholed parking lot, and rusty Dumpster. It was enough trouble keeping her small needlework shop from bankruptcy.

Her cat interrupted her musings by asking "A-row?" from a place between Betsy and the door. Was it time to go to work? the cat wanted to know. Sophie liked the needlework shop and yearned to spend even more hours in it. Up here, she got a little scoop of Iams Less

Active twice a day. Down in the shop, ah, in the shop were potato chips and fragments of chocolate bars and who knew what other treats. Only this last Saturday, she'd garnered a paw-size hunk of bagel spread with strawberry cream cheese, which she'd sneaked into the back room and eaten to the last crumb—a pleasant victory, since her mistress had a distressing habit of snatching delicacies away before the cat got more than one tooth into them. Sophie weighed twenty-two pounds and was as determined to hang on to every ounce as her mistress was to make her svelte.

Yesterday, Sunday, the shop had been closed. Sophie had not had so much as a corner of dry toast. Now, when Betsy put her empty tea mug into the sink, Sophie hurried ahead to the door.

They went down the stairs to the ground floor, around to an obscure door near the back wall, through it, and down a narrow hallway to the back door into the shop. Sophie waited impatiently for her mistress to unlock the door.

Godwin was already in the shop. To Sophie's delight, he had a greasy, cholesterol-laden bacon and egg McMuffin. He was seated at the library table with it and a mug of coffee. While Betsy put the startup cash in the register, Sophie quietly went to touch him on the left shin to let him know where she was. As quietly, Godwin dropped a small piece of buttered muffin with a bit of egg clinging to it, confident it would never touch the carpet.

"Hey, Goddy!" said Betsy, slamming the drawer shut.

"Hmmm?" he said, startled into a too-perfect look of innocence.

"Remind me to call that blacktop company again this morning, will you?"

"Certainly," he said, and when she began to check an order he'd made out, he dropped another morsel.

An hour later, Betsy was putting together a display of small kits consisting of a square of tan or pale green linen; lengths of green, pink, yellow, wine, dark gold, and brown floss; a pattern of tulips in a basket; and a needle. She had made up the kits herself, putting each into a clear plastic bag with daffodils printed on it, tied shut with curly yellow ribbon. She was arranging the kits, priced at seven dollars, in a pretty white basket beside a pot of real tulips and a finished model of the pattern, still in its little Q-snap holder. A stack of little Q-snaps, which had been selling poorly, waited suggestively close to the basket.

Godwin, meanwhile, had clamped a Dazor magnifying light to the library table in the middle of the shop, and was fastening the electric cord to the carpet with long strips of duct tape.

At home on Sunday, Betsy had put together another little basket with illustrations of various stitches, threaded needles, and an assortment of fabrics, so that customers could try these things before buying, or get Godwin's help in doing an elaborate needlepoint stitch. The Dazor was there to help them see more clearly— and if the customer was delighted at how bright and clear things appeared under the Dazor, Betsy had several of the lights all boxed up in the back room.

Betsy had recently visited Zandy's in Burnsville, where the owner had a similar setup. Zandy had told Betsy that she sold at least one Dazor a month. Betsy had sold two Dazors since she took over Crewel World nine months ago. Even at wholesale, the lights were expensive and a burden on the shop's inventory.

Godwin stood up with a grunt, and brushed a fragment of dust from his beautiful lightweight khaki trousers. "That should keep people from tripping," he said. "What's next?"

"Pat Ingle brought a model to me in church on Sunday," said Betsy. "Here it is. We'll need to find space for it on the wall in back."

"Oh, it's The Finery of Nature!" said Godwin, going to look. "Gosh, look at it! Seeing it for real makes me wish I did counted cross stitch myself!"

And that was the purpose of models. Crewel World sold all kinds of needlework, but counted cross stitch patterns needed, more than any other, the impact of the finished product to inspire needleworkers to buy. Betsy had devoted the entire back of her shop to cross-stitch, and the walls there were covered with framed models. But as new patterns arrived and old ones went out of print, a steady trickle of new models was needed.

Betsy used a variety of methods to keep the walls up to date. One was to stitch them herself, but Betsy was still learning the craft and so had to lean heavily on her customers, borrowing finished patterns from them. Sometimes she offered a particularly talented customer free finishing—washing, stretching, and framing, an expensive service—in exchange for the right to display it for a time, or to giving the model maker the materials for a project, plus deep discounts on other patterns and materials, in exchange for doing a particular project.

She had also gained some recent models by a sadder method: Wayzata's Needle Nest had gone out of business, and Pat had sold Betsy some of her models to hang on Crewel World's walls. Fineries of Nature was the last of them.

It was a little after noon when Betsy, looking over a new and complex Terrance Nolan pattern, said, "I wonder if we could get Irene to make a model of this for us."

And as if on cue, the front door went *Bing!* and Irene came in. Irene Potter was one of Betsy's most loyal customers. She was also rude, opinionated, passionate, difficult—and an extraordinarily talented needleworker. A short, thin woman with angry black curls standing up all over her head, she had a narrow face set with very shiny dark eyes. Her clothing came from a Salvation Army store. She wasn't poor, but she put every possible nickel of her income into needlework supplies.

She had a project rolled up under the arm of her shabby winter coat, a faux leopard skin probably thirty years old. "I need your opinion on this," she said without preamble.

"What, on how to finish it?" asked Betsy from behind the big desk that served as a checkout counter.

"No, just an opinion. Yours too," she added over her shoulder, not quite looking at Godwin. This was unusual. Irene had a very accurate notion of Betsy's lack of proficiency but her fear and loathing of Godwin as a gay man normally kept her from acknowledging his expertise in needlework. That most other Crewel World customers thought he had a heightened sense of color and design *because* he was gay cut no ice with Irene.

Godwin, making a comedy of his surprise behind Irene's back, smoothed his face to impassivity as he came to stand beside Betsy. Irene took a deep breath, held it, and unrolled the fabric onto the desk.

Betsy stared; Godwin inhaled sharply. It was an impressionistic painting of a city in a blizzard. The snow blew thickly around the buildings and people, blurring their outlines and the shape of a tall plinth in the center of a square.

But the picture wasn't a painting. It was a highly detailed piece of cross-stitching. "Why, it's wonderful!" exclaimed Betsy. "I've never seen anything like this. Where did you get the pattern, Irene?"

"It's not from a pattern," said Irene. "Martha took me to see the exhibit of American Impressionists at the Art Museum last year. I never could see what was so great about Impressionists; those posters and pictures in magazines look like a mess. But prints are nothing like seeing Impressionist paintings for real."

Betsy nodded. "That's absolutely true, Irene. I didn't get Impressionism either, when all I'd seen were prints. Then I saw my first van Gogh in person and I fell in love. Did you see the Art Museum's exhibit, Goddy?"

"M-hmm." He seemed very absorbed in Irene's piece, moving a step sideways and back, cocking his head at various angles.

Betsy continued, "I don't know why photographs can't tell the truth about Impressionist paintings. Do you, Godwin?"

"It's because they use layers of paint, or lay it on thickly, and use lots of texture, so the light moves across it as you approach. Photographs flatten all that out."

"Yes, I think that's right. This moves with the light, too. It is truly beautiful. Where did you get it, Irene?" Betsy knew she hadn't sold a pattern like this to Irene—

she had never seen a pattern like this, in her shop or anywhere.

"I did it myself," Irene said quietly.

Godwin said, "You did? But your work isn't anything like this!"

Irene gave him a freezing glance and said, "I got to thinking about those paintings, and I went back a second time by myself and I borrowed Martha's copy of the exhibit catalog, and I thought some more, and I did this. Is it any good?"

"It's amazing, it's fantastic," said Betsy.

Godwin said, "It really is wonderful, Irene. How did you get those swirls of snow?" They weren't smooth lines, but lumpish streaks, an effect an oil painter gets by using the edge of his palette knife.

"Caron cotton floss," said Irene. "It's got those slubs in it, and I just kept working it over the top until it looked right." A figure in the foreground, walking with the snow pushing her back into a curve, was done in shades of charcoal and light gray, with a touch of wine at the throat and on a package she was struggling not to lose. The curve of her back, done in broken rows of straight stitches, made the viewer feel her strain against the harsh wind.

Betsy leaned closer. It looked to her as if all the figures and images in the work were done with blended stitches. The overall effect was of solid objects seen through a blur of snow.

Godwin, cocking his head at yet a different angle, frowned and said, "I don't think this is an exact copy of the painting in the exhibit, is it?"

"No," said Irene, as if admitting to a fault. "Mr. Wiggins's painting was old; it had old-fashioned cars and wagons pulled by horses. I used modern cars, except for one of those carriages I've seen in movies that get pulled by a horse through the park. I liked the way Mr. Wiggins's horses looked, so that's why I put one in, too. And I found a photograph in the library of Columbus Circle, so I knew what that tall thing really looks like."

"Plinth," said Godwin. "It's called a plinth."

Irene ignored that. She said to Betsy, "I was afraid it was too . . . messy."

Godwin said, "I think all the overstitching is brilliant."

Betsy said, "Yes, that gives it an especially wonderful effect. What are you going to do with it?"

"Well, I don't know," said Irene. "I wanted to know first if it was any good."

"This is beyond good," said Godwin. "This is . . . this is *art*."

This time Irene glanced at him with respect. "You think so?"

"Yes."

"I agree," said Betsy. "Any art gallery would be proud to offer this. Of course, I'd like you to turn it into a pattern. This would be a real challenge for an advanced stitcher, but I'm sure I could sell it. But maybe you should enter it in a competition first. Is there a competition for work like this, Godwin?"

"There are all sorts of needlework competitions," he said. "It would do well in any of them, I think."

Irene said, "Then I'll put it in the State Fair, I guess." Irene had lots of blue ribbons from the Minnesota State Fair's needlework competitions.

"Or CATS," said Godwin. "Hey, they're coming to

Minneapolis in October this year, so you could enter it in both." CATS was the Creative Arts and Textile Show, which featured needlework designers, classes, and booths selling the latest patterns and fibers. It had a prestigious competition for needlework.

"This is so different from anything I've done before," said Irene, who had in fact never attempted more than slight changes in someone else's pattern, and who had always selected very literal patterns. "But it felt good doing it. It felt better than almost anything I've done before." She reached for the canvas and began to roll it up.

"Don't you want it finished?" asked Betsy.

"No, not yet," said Irene. "Maybe later. I've got to get back to work." She turned and hurried out.

"Probably can't afford to have it finished," said Godwin. "She came in here on Saturday and bought nine colors of wool, two skeins of metallics, and a fat quarter of twenty-eight Cashel. She counted out the last two dollars in change. Poor thing."

Betsy said, "There are a lot of hobbies that pay enough so the hobbyist can at least break even, but this isn't one of them. Needleworkers can't sell their work for even what the materials cost, much less the hours spent stitching it. That piece she just took out, she'll probably end up giving away rather than be insulted by an offer of forty dollars for it. I just don't understand why fabulously talented people who work with needles and fibers don't get the recognition that people who work in oil or metal do. It isn't fair."

"Would you buy it?" asked Godwin.

Betsy half closed her eyes, picturing it on her living room wall, in a smooth, dark frame . . . "Gosh, yes."

"What would you pay for it? I mean, if it was an auction, and you were bidding on it. How high would you go?"

Again Betsy half closed her eyes, imagining raising her hand with a numbered paddle in it. Fifty dollars, a hundred dollars, two hundred dollars. "Who's bidding against me?" she asked.

"The Getty."

Betsy giggled. "Then I haven't got a chance, have I? But I'd go as high as five hundred, I guess."

Godwin smacked his hand down on the desk. "Sold! Would you really go that high?"

Betsy hesitated, then recalled that figure in the foreground so realistically bent under the wind's constant shove, and the way the snow swirled around the plinth and softened the vertical lines of the buildings. She had worked not far from Columbus Circle many years ago, and had once been out in a city blizzard . . . "Actually, yes, I think I would. But I'd also like to hang it down here as a model for a while, and sell lots of patterns. Oh, darn, I let Irene get away without asking if she'd do that Terry Nolan model for me. Remind me when we're closing up, I need to call her at home."

It was a little after one when the door's *Bing!* brought Alice and Martha in, project bags in hand. It was nearly time for the Monday Bunch to meet. The two went to the library table in the middle of the room, but hesitated when they saw the Dazor light.

"What's this?" asked Alice, a tall woman with mannish shoulders and chin.

"It's a magnifying light, silly," said Martha, who was short and plump, with silver hair.

"I know that. What I meant was, what's it doing here?"

Betsy said, "I've set up a sample basket so people can try out fabrics and fibers and stitches, and I'm going to let them do it under the Dazor if they like, so they can see better."

Alice, who was inclined to blurt out whatever was on her mind, said, "And maybe somehow they'll get the notion they need the lamp, too?"

"Alice!" scolded Martha. A brisk-mannered widow in her late seventies, she was an ardent practitioner of Minnesota Nice.

"That's the idea, certainly," agreed Betsy cheerfully.

The women had barely taken their places at the library table when the door opened again. This time it was Jill Cross, a tall, ash-blond woman with a Gibson girl face. She nodded at Betsy and Godwin and took a seat at the table.

"Not on duty today?" asked Alice in her deep voice.

"No," said Jill, opening her drawstring bag and taking out a needlepoint canvas pinned to a wooden frame. It was a Peter Ashe painting of a Russian church liberally ornamented with fanciful domes. She was using a gold metallic on the one swirled like a Dairy Queen cone.

"That's coming along real nice," noted Alice.

"Uh-huh." Jill was normally taciturn, but this shortness bordered on rudeness.

Betsy said, "Something bothering you?"

"Huh? Oh." She sighed. "All right, yes. I think I told at least some of you that Lars was going to sell his hobby farm."

"You told me," said Martha. "I thought you were

pleased. I know you've been wanting him to cut back on the time he spends trying to make a go of that place."

"Yes, that's true. Actually, he's had it for sale for a month now."

"What, you're afraid he isn't going to get his price for it?" asked Alice.

"No, he got his price last week."

"Then what's the problem?" asked Martha.

"I think he's already spent the money."

"On what?" asked Betsy. She knew Lars and Jill had been dating for a long time—two or even three years. They weren't living together, or even officially engaged, but neither dated anyone else so far as Betsy knew.

"That's just it, I don't know. He's been making long-distance calls and reading books about—something. You know Lars, working fifty hours a week isn't enough to keep that man occupied. First it was boats, then it was the hobby farm. I don't know what's next, flying lessons or do-it-yourself dentistry. That's what's bothering me—he never talks to me before he decides what he's going to do."

Godwin said, "Some men are just terrible at sharing their plans. Afraid they'll start an argument, I guess."

"Are you having trouble with John again?" asked Alice, sometimes as perceptive as she was tactless.

"No, not exactly. Well, actually, it's me who doesn't want to start the argument." Godwin lived with a wealthy attorney, an older man who, by Godwin's telling, was kind, generous, and very possessive.

Alice, who had sat down next to the Dazor, made a sudden exclamation.

"What?" asked Betsy.

Alice had casually turned the light on and, instead of using it to light her crochet project, had taken a scrap of twenty-count Jobelan from the basket to look at it through the big magnifying glass. "I can *see* this!" she said.

"So can I," said Godwin, who was at the other end of the table from her.

"No, I mean, I can see the weave, I can actually see the weave!"

Betsy and Godwin exchanged smiles. While Alice was not in a position to afford a Dazor, her reaction was exactly what they'd hoped for. Other customers would sit there and hold a piece of high-count linen under that magnifying light, and the cash register would ring merrily.

Two more Monday Bunch members came in to sit down with projects and soon the table was alive with helpful hints and gossip. Betsy kept the coffee cups filled, served the occasional customer, and brought patterns, fabrics, and fibers to the table to be examined and, often enough, set aside by the cash register.

She came from the back with the newest Mirabilia pattern to hear Martha saying in an amused voice, "Honestly, Emily acts as if hers is the first baby ever born! All she ever talks about anymore is the joy and burden of staying home with an infant."

"All first-time mothers are like that," said Kate McMahon with a little sigh. "My Susan certainly is, and I expect I was, too."

"Have any of you talked to Irene lately?" asked Betsy, anxious on behalf of Alice to change the subject. Alice's only child had died young of a heart ailment.

"No, why?" asked Phil Galvin, a retired railroad engineer. He was working on a counted cross stitch pattern of a mountain goat.

"She has made the most amazing—"

The door to the shop made its annoying *Bing!* sound, and a very big police officer came in. He was about twenty-five, golden blond, and excited. "Found you at last, Jill!" he exclaimed, his voice as loud as he was big.

"Hi, Lars!" said Jill, getting up and heading toward him. "What's up?"

"Look at this, look what I found!" He had a sheaf of papers in his hand and thrust it at her.

Jill took the papers, glanced at the top one, then more slowly looked at two or three sheets under it. "What is this? Some kind of old car—what, reported stolen?" she asked. "Where'd it turn up?"

"No, no! I finally found this for sale. I can't believe the price. Wait till you see it!"

"See it?" asked Jill, handing back the papers. "What do you mean, what have you bought?"

Lars thrust the papers back at her. "In there, look at the picture of it!"

Betsy, curious, came to look around Jill's shoulder.

"You want to *buy* this?" said Jill, having sifted through the papers until she found the eight-by-ten color photo again. "Why?"

But Betsy, glancing at the printing on the margin of the photo, said, "Oh, my God, it's a Stanley Steamer! Is it for real? Does it run? Where is it?"

"Yes, it's real, a 1911 touring car. It's in Albuquerque. And yes, it runs, or he's pretty sure it will, after it has a little work done on it. He had an accident with it a few years ago and it's been just sitting under a tarp in his back yard. But he says they're harder to kill than a rattlesnake. What I can't believe is the price. Only wants seventeen thousand for it!"

"*Dollars?*" said Jill. "For an old, *old* car that's been in a *wreck* and it will *maybe* run after you've done, oh yeah, a *little* work on it?"

"You're really going to bring it up here?" asked Betsy eagerly.

"Of course he isn't!" barked Jill. "Steam?" she said to Lars. "Like a locomotive?"

"Yeah, just like a locomotive, except it's a car. Isn't that great? It's got the original boiler in it!"

"From *1911*? A ninety-year-old boiler sounds dangerous to me."

"The boiler on a Stanley never blows. Ever. And there are lots of them still out there on the road. There's a whole organization of people who drive them. And there's all kinds of places that make parts for it, tires and windshields and all. The owner is an old guy, a doctor, who can't work on it himself anymore, he's got heart problems." He shifted his ardent gaze to Betsy, whose expression was much more receptive than his girlfriend's. "I found this old book by a guy who got a hold of a Stanley and got it running. He tells some stories in that book that about had me rolling on the floor." Thinking about the stories in the book made his blue eyes twinkle and the corners of his mouth turn up. Lars was a good-looking man, and when amused and enthusiastic, he was irresistible.

Betsy said, "Will you take me for a ride in your Stanley Steamer, Lars?"

Jill turned away and walked back to the table, where

she put a great deal of meaning into the way she sat down.

Lars didn't notice. He continued eagerly to Betsy, "Nobody knows how fast the Stanley Steamer can go, 'cause as long as you hold the throttle open, it just keeps on accelerating. In 1906 it set the world land speed record of a hundred and twenty-seven miles an hour. There's a picture of it in this guy's book of the special chassis they put on it, like a canoe. In 1907 they tried again—it was on Daytona Beach in Florida—and this time, at over a hundred and fifty, it hit a bump and the air got under it, and it actually took off, like an airplane!" Lars's hand described a shallow arc. "Of course, it crashed after a few dozen yards, but just think, over hundred and fifty, and that *still* wasn't its top speed!"

"In 1907? That's amazing!"

Lars continued, "Most cars back then could manage about twenty-five miles an hour going downhill with a tail wind, so it isn't amazing, it's *fantastic*! I wonder if my car can go that fast." His blue eyes turned dreamy.

"But then it crashed," murmured Jill, bowing her head. "Lord, help us not to forget that little part, amen."

Several other members of the Monday Bunch snickered softly.

Lars, aware at last that he had lost Jill, went to her to show her the color photo again. He said in a wheedling voice, "Just look at it. It's beautiful, isn't it? Look at the shape, so beautiful and old and classy. It's got brass trim and wooden wheels, and look at those big old lamps for headlights. Plus, it doesn't have a horn like other cars, but a whistle!" Lars shrilled a creditable imitation of a steam train whistle. *"Wheee-owwwwww!*

And it doesn't go brrum, brrum like gasoline engines. It goes *chuff, chuff, chuff, chuff*!" He began to circle the library table, elbows bent and arms working. "*Chuff, chuff, chuff—whee, whee-owwwwwww!*"

Phil and the women laughed.

Jill, her voice sounding strained from her attempt to be reasonable, said, "Listen to me, Lars. This car has got to be dangerous. It's more than ninety years old, and it's been in a wreck. And it's a steam-powered automobile. That's something they tried and gave up on, or why isn't every car on the road today powered by steam? And look at this thing, it hasn't even got a roof! What are you going to do when winter comes?"

"Oh, it's not going to be my main car. I'm just going to drive it for fun!"

Phil, never one to spoil a good argument, said, "I could help you get it going, Lars. I started out in steam-driven locomotives."

"See?" Lars said to Jill.

Phil continued, "And there's an antique car meet every year right here in Minnesota. They drive from New London to New Brighton."

"New Brighton?" echoed Betsy. "You mean *our* New Brighton? The Minneapolis suburb?"

Phil nodded. "They finish up in a park in New Brighton, and the mayor comes to shake every driver's hand. I've gone a couple of times to watch them come in. I remember there's usually a 1901 Oldsmobile, and a 1908 Cadillac, and a spread of Maxwells and Fords. Beautiful old cars—and one year they had those bicycles that have a big wheel up front and a little bitty wheel behind. There's a big club that runs the thing. People come from all over to drive in it."

"Are they the Minnesota Transportation Museum people?" asked Martha. "We've got some of them right here in town."

"No, those folks run the street cars and steamboat and a couple of steam locomotives," said Phil. "This is a different bunch, they only run horseless carriages."

"An annual meet, huh?" said Lars thoughtfully. "Naw, they probably wouldn't let me in it with my Stanley. I'd be passing them old explosion-engine people right and left." He began to circle the table again. *"Chuff, chuff, chuff, wheee-owwww!"* he crowed, working his elbows back and forth. "Get a horse!" He huffed back to Jill and got onto one knee so he could look up appealingly at her. "Ride with me?"

Jill frowned and looked away—only to encounter Betsy's equally ardent face. "I'll help. In fact, I'll be Lars's sponsor. I'll pay fees and buy coal or wood, or whatever you burn to make steam. Mention the name of the shop and I'll split the cost of restoration. Let me ride along, and it won't cost him a dime. Say yes, Jill, please?"

Jill sighed and looked again at the photo, shaking her head. Betsy looked too, holding her breath, wishing hard. The car was standing on a tarred road against the backdrop of desert scrub and cactus. It gleamed a rich forest green. The wooden wheel spokes were painted yellow, and there appeared to be yellow pinstriping on the body. And Jill was wrong, it did have a top, if that folded hunk of black canvas hanging out over the back seat was any guide.

Something that looked like an old-fashioned vacuum cleaner, complete with hose, was curled up against the passenger's—no, the steering wheel was on the right, so against the driver's side, under the door.

"Strange the photographer didn't notice when he took the picture that there was a vacuum cleaner still on the running board," Betsy remarked. The car was gleaming on the outside, so she assumed the inside had also been cleaned and polished.

"It's not a vacuum cleaner, it's for when you stop to take on water," said Lars, rising to point at the device with a big forefinger. "It just sucks it up out of a well or a pond or even a ditch. But you can pull into some- one's yard and use their hose, too."

"Wow!" said Betsy, thinking how thrilling it would be to have a Stanley Steamer chuff up in front of the shop to ask for a bucket of water. How even more mar- velous to be riding in a Stanley. What a thrill!

But Jill didn't smile, and Lars, realizing at last how deep in the doghouse he was, knelt again. "I know I should have talked to you before I decided to buy it," he said. "And if you say no, I'll call back and tell him I've changed my mind."

Betsy closed her eyes and crossed her fingers.

She heard Martha say, "I've always wanted to ride in an antique car."

Then Alice said, "We could make costumes. Waists and long skirts, and great big hats with veils."

Godwin said, "We could find boaters and celluloid collars, and make spats and close-fitting trousers! Oh you kid!"

Betsy hadn't thought about costumes. Oh, Jill just couldn't say no!

Phil added, "I could renew my boiler license easy, if it would make you feel better about this."

"Please?" said Betsy.

Jill let out a long breath. "Oh, what the heck. I'm not living dangerously enough already, arresting drunk drivers and the occasional murderer Betsy scares up. So sure, Lars honey, go tell the doctor with the bad heart you'll take his crumpled car off his hands."

2

A few weeks later, Betsy was preparing to close Crewel World for the night. It was a little after five. The last customer had just left. She ran the cash register, made sure there were no sales slips loose on the desk, took forty dollars out of the register to keep as opening-up money for tomorrow, signed the deposit slip Godwin had made out and sent him off with it and the day's profits.

Then she hurried upstairs to give Sophie her evening meal, put the money into a locked drawer, and change into wool slacks and a heavy sweater. She grabbed her raincoat and a knit hat, dashed back down the stairs and out the back way to her car.

Lars had called in the afternoon to say that he was back with the Stanley, and did she want a ride? She'd been so excited she nearly forgot to ask him for directions to his new place.

It was less than five minutes away, out St. Alban's Bay Road a mile and a half, to Weekend Street, a narrow lane about three houses long. Lars, having concluded the sale of his hobby farm, had rented a very modest cottage at the bottom of the lane. It was surrounded by middle-size trees and a lot of brush, but it had a big yard. A driveway led behind the house to a small red barn.

Beside the barn was a long, low, white trailer, like a multihorse trailer, except this one had no windows. It was hitched to Lars's dirty blue pickup truck, which apparently hadn't gone to the buyer of his farm.

Betsy steered her car onto the weedy lawn, got out, and went through the open double doors of the barn. Close up, the barn was relatively new, sided vertically with aluminum "boards" and floored with cement. The oil stains on the floor and the big electric winch that ran on an overhead rail announced that this shed was no stranger to people who worked on engines. A workbench along one wall had a vise on it and a pegboard above it with the outline of numerous tools, though the tools presently on it didn't always match the outlines.

Lars and Jill were both there. Jill, in jeans and windbreaker, had her hands in her back pockets and a worried look in her eye. Lars was just grinning.

The backside of the old car was higher than their heads, a rich, gleaming green. There was no rear bumper, and the single taillight, near the left fender, was a brass oil lamp with a round red eye.

The tires seemed tall, perhaps because they were narrow. Betsy asked, "What if you get a flat? Do you have a spare?"

Lars said, "No, the spare's on it. I'm going to have to order a new tire. But I hope it never gets a flat. They have inner tubes and they're harder than hell to change. But these are fine, and they last a long time," he added hastily, not wanting to discourage his patron.

He went to wheel a long, narrow, many-drawered steel chest out of the way so Betsy could walk around the car. "He sold me the tool chest, too."

Jill muttered, "*Takes* lots of tools, I see."

"No, it doesn't," retorted Lars. "No more than most old cars, anyhow. It's just that some of them are . . . different."

"How did he wreck it?" asked Betsy, coming to the damaged fender and noting that the big brass headlight was smashed as well. She thought the bulb had been torn out until she saw the other headlight didn't have a bulb, either. They must not make the kind of bulbs it took anymore.

"Last time he had it out, he was run off the road by a gawker. You got to watch for those gawkers, he told me. Anyhow, the wreck triggered a heart attack, so he figured he'd better sell."

"Can you get new headlights, too? I see there aren't any bulbs in these."

"They don't come with bulbs, they're acetylene. But they aren't very bright, so we don't run at night."

"Can you start it?" asked Betsy, coming the rest of the way around it. "I mean, right now? Or is there something wrong with the motor, too?"

"It runs fine," Lars said firmly, glancing at Jill. "Dr. Fine taught me how to start it and had me do it alone a couple of times. It's not hard, but you can't do it fast. His personal record for getting it powered up was seventeen and a half minutes."

Lars got out the owner's manual and consulted it, then checked to make sure there was water and the two kinds of fuel in adequate amounts. The car had several gauges, but not, apparently, a fuel gauge. Lars used a wooden ruler dipped into the tanks to determine fuel levels. "It holds twenty-five gallons of water, seventeen gallons of unleaded gas, and two gallons of Coleman gas, plus a gallon of steam oil, which is a blend of four-hundred-weight oil and tallow."

"Four hund—" began Jill, but was interrupted by Betsy's exclamation: *"Tallow?"*

"Uh-huh." Lars, having produced a handheld propane torch from the tool box, was twisting the knob. The torch began to hiss and he lit it with a cigarette lighter. "Y'see, this isn't an internal combustion engine, it's a steam engine, so the rules are different. She runs real hot, so you need a lubricant that can take it. He says you get used to the new rules, and they're good ones, and real safe, only different. Dr. Fine says there's people in Wisconsin who own Stanleys, and they can help me. Plus there's a big club I'm gonna join, it's international, so there's a good support group."

Jill remarked to the ceiling, "Unlike AA, these people help you stay with the sickness, not get clean."

"What?" said Lars. Adjusting the flame of his torch, he hadn't been paying attention.

"Nothing, nothing," said Betsy, waving a shushing hand at Jill. "Go on, Lars."

"Anyhow, this club can tell me where I can get the stuff I need to keep her running." He put a big, caressing hand on the intact front fender, then went to the back of the car and turned a flat steel knob on a copper tank. Then he went to the front—Betsy and Jill following—and began playing the torch through a pair of silver-dollar-size holes at the base of the hood, which, Betsy suddenly noticed, was shaped like a fat oval, not flat on the sides like ordinary cars.

"What are you doing?" she asked.

"Getting the pilot light started."

Betsy laughed uncertainly, but Lars said, "I have to get it hot before I can turn on the gasoline."

After a few minutes, satisfied that the pilot light was operating properly, Lars got into the car. He opened another valve, then began to pump a long handle back and forth. "Getting the gasoline started," he explained.

He got out again and showed Betsy the two small, recurved nozzles that came from under the car and ran into the holes he'd been playing the torch into. "Feel," he said, running a finger across one of the nozzles.

Betsy complied, but yanked her hand away from the strong, fine spray. "What's that, water?"

"No, gasoline."

Betsy sniffed her fingertip and was shocked to realize Lars was right. "You mean it just sprays out in the open like that?"

"Sure. It has to mix with the air as it goes into those two holes."

"That can't be safe!" exclaimed Jill. "Spraying gasoline like that, you'll get a vapor that will explode."

"No, you get a vapor that will burn," said Lars.

"Why doesn't it mix in the cylinder—" Betsy stopped.

"Because then it would be an internal combustion engine," Lars confirmed with a grin.

Suddenly a low, eerie *whoooooooooooo* began to sound from the car. Jill grabbed Betsy by the arm and ran her out of the barn. When they looked around and Lars wasn't behind them, Jill shouted, "Get out! Get out! It's going to blow!"

"No, it isn't!" called Lars, his voice filled with laughter. "It's called singing! She sings when she's building a head of steam!"

"Cool!" said Betsy, shrugging her elbow loose from Jill's grip. She would have gone back, but Jill took her by the arm again.

Lars came out to the doorway. "Soon as we get to four hundred and fifty pounds of pressure, we can head on down the road."

"Four hundred and fifty pounds!" Jill exclaimed, then murmured in Betsy's ear, "Don't go, don't go."

But Betsy again shrugged free and this time did go back inside to watch as Lars continued the process of starting up, tapping a gauge on the dashboard, pumping up the gasoline, nodding as he checked his owner's manual; and was reassured by the big man's happy confidence. After all, he'd gone through all this just a couple of days ago, and surely he'd notice if things were going differently. Right?

It took about twenty minutes. The "song" of the boiler slowly rose in tone, then stopped. Lars opened the passenger side door, clambered over into the driver's seat, and said, "All aboard!"

Jill warned, "You are crazy, Betsy, if you get into that contraption with him."

But Betsy stepped up onto the running board, feeling

the springiness of the suspension, then up again into the passenger seat of tufted black leather. "This is so high!" she said. She automatically began feeling around for a seat belt, then laughed at herself. "Let's go, Lars!"

"You sure you're not coming?" Lars asked Jill, who in reply backed onto the grass and waved them off.

The car had not made a sound since it left off "singing," and there was not the faintest vibration to show that a motor was running. As Betsy watched, Lars depressed two small pedals crowded together on the floor, and then slowly moved a silver lever up a slice-of-pie metal holder on the steering column.

With a quiet *chuff, chuff* the car moved smoothly backward. Lars steered it to the left, moved the lever downward, and pushed on the third pedal on the floor. The car stopped.

"Yay!" he cheered softly, and Betsy realized he was a little nervous after all. He grinned and waved at Jill then moved the lever up the pie slice, and the car, this time in absolute silence, went down the driveway to Weekend Lane and up to St. Alban's Bay Road. Lars braked nearly to a stop at the road, then turned left. As they moved out, he became bolder and moved the throttle lever up a little more. The car, still making no noise at all, began to gain speed.

"Wow!" cheered Betsy. *"Wow!"* There was no vibration, no chuff-chuffing, just smooth acceleration.

Lars, his grin broadening, winked at her and pulled a lever under the steering wheel. A very loud whistley racket let loose. Steam roiled up all around them. Betsy would have jumped out of the car, but Lars grabbed her by the shoulder. "Ha, ha!" he cheered, and blew the whistle again.

This time Betsy yelled in delight. It was safe, this was great! Coming to a stop sign, Lars braked, but the car didn't slow. He slammed the throttle down, and tramped hard on the brake, but they were only slowing as they entered the intersection. He pulled the wheel hard right and they leaned very dangerously going around the corner. Despite the narrow tires, the car didn't slide or skid and Betsy grabbed the gasoline pump lever to keep from being thrown out. Once onto the even narrower road, the car righted itself.

"Wow!" exclaimed Betsy yet again, and Lars laughed and reopened the throttle.

There were trees crowding close on either side, the last bits of sun twinkling through the branches. The upright windshield blocked the wind, rapidly cooling as the sun went down, so she felt quite comfortable.

"Yah-hooo!" Lars cheered and blew the whistle as he pushed the lever up a little more. In a smooth, continuing silence the car answered the call, speeding up effortlessly. It was weird, it was surprising, it was wonderful.

Betsy began to laugh; she couldn't help it. It was like the first time she'd gone sailing.

Lars began to experiment with the car, slowing to a crawl, accelerating to about forty—there was no speedometer—slowing again. As he came nearly to a stop, he stomped suddenly on the pair of pedals, and the car jumped instantly backward with a little squeal of rubber. He lifted his foot and the car jumped right into forward again. "Look, Ma!" he said. "No transmission!"

"What—you didn't break something, did you?" asked Betsy.

"No, no, no. The Stanley brothers invented a steam

car with a transmission, but sold the rights, so when they wanted to try steam again, they had to figure a way around the patents. They couldn't get around the transmission patent, so they invented a car without a transmission. The motor turns the axle directly, no gears. The engine turns over once, the wheels go around once."

"Uh-huh," said Betsy, not sure if this was brilliant or troublesome.

A hill, not high but fairly steep, was ahead, but the car forged up it with no hesitation. "See? Torque to burn!" cheered Lars.

And Betsy, who happened to know a little about engineering because her father had been an engineer, realized that the lack of gearing was the reason for the torque. Brilliant, she decided.

Around another corner, they were on Excelsior Boulevard, which ran parallel to Highway 7. The highway was crowded with commuters on their way home from work, but several dared to slow down when they saw the Stanley, and two or three honked.

Betsy waved happily at them, and Lars showed off a little bit by blowing the whistle, causing an unaware driver to swerve dangerously. The road was flat and clear along this stretch. They came to Christmas Lake Road, which crossed Highway 7 and joined Excelsior Boulevard. Commuters who lived in Excelsior were backed up on the highway, waiting to make the turn. They crowded onto Excelsior when the light changed. There was only a stop sign for Lars, and he seemed in no hurry to bully his way into the stream of traffic. Waiting for the traffic to clear, he checked his gauges.

"See the winker?" he said, pointing to a small red

button light blinking rapidly. "If that stops winking, it means we're running low on oil." Betsy watched it for a while, but it never stopped winking.

Cars coming off the highway slowed for a look, causing others to honk impatiently. One, steering where he looked, swayed toward them, and Lars blew his whistle angrily, nearly hiding the Stanley in the steam and setting off a chorus of honks. Betsy stood and waved her fist at the driver, but was laughing too hard to make her threat worth anything.

Then there came a gap and they went on down the road, past the sudden steep hill of the cemetery, around a curve, and past the police station, then Adele's Ice Cream and the McDonald's. At the next stop sign they turned right and were back on St. Alban's. The circuit, about three miles, had taken less than fifteen minutes.

The view along St. Alban's Bay Road was more open but no less pleasant, with Excelsior Bay on their left and St. Alban's Bay on their right. They went onto a two-lane bridge over the narrow link between them. Some people had already put their boats in the water, though it was a little early for pleasure sailing. Over the bridge was a yacht and boat sales and repair company, then a row of mixed small cottages and bigger houses, some hidden behind hedges, others open, with grass showing green and tulips budding. The trees on either side had leaves almost big enough to hide their branches. Betsy sniffed, testing the spring air, but the car had a strong aroma of its own, an unpleasant combination of gasoline, kerosene, and hot oil. But now, quite suddenly, the scent of gasoline was overwhelming. She turned to ask Lars about it and saw the look of alarm forming on his face.

He shut the throttle down and began to brake. "I hope this isn't what I think it is," he muttered. He reached for a valve knob, pulling onto the narrow, sloping shoulder, fighting the wheel one-handed as the tires gripped hard at the loose gravel.

As they slowed nearly to a stop, he turned to say, "Get—" but was interrupted by an enormous fiery explosion. Betsy flung her arms up and screamed. Smoke, dark flames, and gas fumes filled the air.

The fat oval hood was standing up, and black smoke was pouring out. Betsy was standing in the middle of the road looking at the car, with no memory of climbing down.

And then there were people running toward them.

A car going by swerved sharply to miss Betsy. It pulled onto the shoulder and the man driving it got out and ran toward them, his face alarmed. A passenger got out, cell phone to his ear, gesturing as he spoke.

Betsy suddenly realized she was deaf.

But she felt no pain. She was not scattered in small pieces over the surrounding area. She was not on fire or even burned. Or bleeding.

Lars was standing behind the Stanley cranking down a valve. He was calm, intact, and not on fire.

In fact, the car seemed to be intact, the smoke almost cleared away.

"What the hell happened?" shouted the driver of the stopped car as he came up to them, sounding to Betsy as if he were speaking from under a thick blanket. Lars said something back, which Betsy could not hear at all.

The man repeated his question, and Lars came out from behind the Stanley. "The pilot light went out!" he shouted.

Betsy began to laugh. It was a sick, hysterical laugh, and Lars hurried over to take her by the shoulders and shake her. "Hey!" he said. "Hey! Stop it!"

Betsy managed to stop, and put her hands on Lars's arms to make him quit shaking her. "I—I'm oh-okay," Betsy managed between teeth that were suddenly chattering. Her touch on Lars turned to a grasp, as her knees began to give way.

Several people came close, and one said, "Shall I call 911?"

Everyone's voice was becoming audible, if muffled. Betsy touched one ear with the palm of her hand.

The man with the cell phone said, "I already did!"

"What did you do that for?" demanded Lars angrily.

Betsy heard a sound and turned back toward town. Was that the volunteer fire department siren? By the way the others were looking toward it, it was. She moved her jaw in a kind of yawn, trying to get her hearing the rest of the way back.

Lars said angrily, "Call and cancel! The car's fine, and we're fine!"

That was met with disbelieving silence.

"No, really," said Betsy, "I'm all right. I'm not injured." She looked at the Stanley, which seemed innocent of all wrongdoing, though the hood still stood upright. "But my God, Lars, if that's what happens when the pilot light goes out, what happens when you run out of steam?" And she started laughing again.

"Hey," he began, but she stepped back out of his reach.

"I'm fine," she repeated, and in fact her knees seemed to have regained their strength. "Better see to your car."

"Oh, it's okay, really, it's in perfect condition. We'll

let the fumes air out and relight the pilot light, and we're back on our way." He walked over to the front of the car and began looking at the squat white round thing where the engine in an ordinary car would be.

"What the hell kind of a car is that?" asked a stocky young man near the front of the small crowd.

A skinny old man said, "I believe it's a Stanley Steamer."

Betsy said, surprised, "You're absolutely right. How did you know that?"

"My grandfather had one. Kept it in an old shed back of the barn. He used to fire it up and let me drive it over the pastures. It could climb out of the deepest ditch on the place. Ran her on diesel fuel and kerosene, if I remember rightly. But I burned the boiler dry a couple of times and it wouldn't run after that."

He was speaking to the crowd as well as to Betsy. Lars had walked around to the side of the car to lift the front seat and rummage around among what sounded like heavy metal tools.

"What are you going to do?" the man with the cell phone asked him.

Lars came up with a flashlight and a length of stiff wire. "Gonna clean out the pilot light," he said. "*If* all of you will give me some room!" He spoke with annoyance weighted by the unmistakable authority of a police officer, and everyone decided to give him all the room he wanted.

"I used to use a coat hanger," the old man said, and he was immediately surrounded by people who wanted to hear more about coat hangers and Stanley Steamers.

Betsy went to stand behind Lars, trying to see without interfering in what he was doing. She heard a car horn honking and honking and turned to see a big old Buick roaring up the road. "Here comes Jill," she said.

Lars groaned. "She's gonna make me sell it, I just know she is!" And then he groaned louder at the sound of a siren approaching. Several sirens.

The man who had waved the cell phone said, "I called and canceled! Honest!" Then he hurried into the passenger seat of his car and left.

The Buick slid to a stop across the road and Jill emerged, her face white. "What happened?" she demanded.

"The pilot light went out," said Betsy, shrugging in further ignorance.

"Pilot light—?"

Lars said, slamming down the hood, "When the pilot light goes out, gasoline fumes collect, and if the boiler's hot enough, it sets them off. You get a little bang, the hood flies up, the fumes escape, and you're fine."

Jill said, "I heard that 'little bang' three quarters of a mile from here. I imagine all of Excelsior, most of Shorewood, and half of Deephaven heard it. The 911 switchboard must've lit up like a Christmas tree." She gestured back up the road at the approaching emergency vehicles, their sirens drowning out anything further she might have said.

The fire truck crew listened while Lars explained what was going on, the ambulance crew gave Betsy a cursory examination—Lars refused to let them examine him—and at last they departed. Most of the neighbors by then had gone back into their houses, though the old man hung out at a safe distance to watch Lars work.

Lars spent fifteen minutes clearing the pilot light tube, then reopened the valve to let Coleman gas reach it, lit a long weed stem, and squatted to poke it through one of the holes in the front of the hood. There was a *whump* that shot flame out both holes. Lars fell backward, landing on his hands and bottom, but said, "See? It's fine, she's starting up for me!" He kept his head turned awkwardly away from Jill, and Betsy, in a pretense of going to see if her hat was in the car, saw the reason. The latest explosion had left a blister in place of Lars's right eyebrow. But the burner was hissing happily, and Lars continued the process of rebuilding a head of steam, which took almost no time, as the boiler hadn't cooled much during the breakdown.

Jill insisted Betsy ride with her, that Lars drive very slowly; and she followed behind him, emergency lights blinking, all the way home.

3

In a Minnesota summer, nights can be gloriously cool. At 4 A.M. Saturday, June 12, in a dead calm, the temperature was sixty-three. By six it had risen to sixty-eight, and as the sun climbed, it continued to rise. A light breeze started flapping the pennants on the sailboats moored at private docks in St. Alban's and Excelsior Bay.

The breeze caused the sailor heading out on Lake Minnetonka to reach for his jacket, but by the time he passed the Big Island, he had taken it off again. By 8 A.M., under a spotless sky, it was seventy-one.

Already the air around The Common, Excelsior's lakeshore park, had begun to smell of grilled pork, hot dogs, cotton candy, smoothies, and deep-fried chicken tenders. Rows of white canvas booths were rising like geometrical mushrooms, filled to bursting with paintings, jewelry, sculpture, Japanese kites, birdhouses shaped like English cottages, and other exotica, as artists prepared for business. Excelsior's annual art fair was hoisting canvas as it prepared to get under way.

The weatherman predicted temperatures in the upper eighties by midafternoon, but added that the continued light breeze off the lake would keep everyone at the fair comfortable.

Betsy came out of her shop around nine. The long block of Lake Street that Crewel World faced was empty of cars, but had a white canvas booth of its own set up in the middle of the street. Betsy headed for it. There were three people in the booth, a man and two women. Above the booth was a plastic banner with AN-TIQUE CAR RUN printed on it in rust-brown letters.

The real Antique Car Run, from New London to New Brighton, was next weekend. Today, Saturday, a group of twenty-five drivers were in the Twin Cities on a publicity tour that included a run from the state capitol building in St. Paul to Excelsior and back.

It was rumored the governor would ride in one of the cars, a rumor the club was careful not to extinguish. Minnesota's eccentric governor always drew a crowd.

Both women in the booth were on cell phones, and both were gesturing so wildly that Betsy, approaching, felt a pang of alarm. But the man, a nice-looking fellow about Betsy's age, winked at her and said, "They're always like this just before things get under way."

Betsy said, "Things are going according to plan, then."

"Yes, the first car will leave in about five minutes."

"Where do you want me?"

"Right here. But we don't have anything for you to

do until the first ones arrive, which won't be for about two hours. Your tasks will be to note the time of arrival of each vehicle, and to point them at me in the booth so I can direct them to parking places along the curb." He glanced up and down the empty street, which had No Parking signs tied to every pole. "I hear we're not very popular with the committee running the Art Fair."

Betsy turned to look up toward The Common, two blocks away. Starting before dawn, a slow-moving line of vans, SUVs, trucks, and campers bearing artists and their work had clogged this street, the last draining away into the fair only an hour ago. But now the street belonged to the Antique Car Run, so none of the many hundreds of visitors to the fair could park here today. This distressed those running the art fair, because every extra block visitors had to walk to the lakefront meant their feet would give out that much sooner, giving that much less time for the artists to extract money.

No, Deb Hart had *not* been pleased at a meeting of her art fair committee and the Antique Car Run committee.

In vain the Antique Car Run president had argued that people who came to see the horseless carriages would then wander over to the fair so temptingly nearby.

Deb had argued that people who came to look at old cars were not the same kind of people who visited art fairs. She had suggested a parade of old cars up Excelsior's main street, all the way up to the far other end, where there was plenty of room and no competition from fair goers. "Besides," she'd pointed out in a reasonable voice, "there's the car dealership down there, which is probably more in tune with the kind of people who turn out for an event like yours."

But Mayor Jamison had sided with the antique car event planners. "There are all kinds of car people," he had said, "hot rod people, classic car people, new car people. But horseless carriage people are different. They're not interested in tires and cubic-inch measurements of engines, but the history and unique beauty of these early machines. Such people see their antiques as works of art rather than mechanical devices, and so might more properly be classed among the art seekers who come to the fair."

Betsy, who had endured much ear-bending from Lars about main burner jets, valve plungers, and cylinder oil, had not slipped into prevarication by so much as a nod of agreement with the mayor. Instead, she bit her tongue, while Deb Hart, all unknowing, succumbed to the mayor's argument.

Now, on this beautiful June morning, she looked at the empty street and said, "No, the art fair is not happy with us." Then she went back to the shop, unlocked the door, and stood a moment, thinking how she was going to accomplish her next task, which was to get the quilt stand just inside her door out onto the sidewalk.

Last night, a little before closing, an elderly woman named Mildred Feeney had come in asking for Betsy. She said she was associated with the Antique Car Run and asked if she might store a quilt that was to be a prize in a raffle in Betsy's shop "just for tonight," and Betsy had agreed. She had also agreed to bring it out in the morning. But that was before she'd seen the quilt and the stand on which it was to be displayed. She'd been busy in the back while it was brought in, appar-

ently by a big crew of husky men, because now, looking
at it, she wondered how on earth she was going to bring
it out again all by herself.

The quilt, a queen-size model, was draped over a
large wooden frame shaped like an upside down V. The
frame was large enough to accommodate the quilt un-
folded, holding it several inches clear of the floor on
both sides.

And the stand wasn't on wheels. Betsy took one end
with both hands, tried to lift it, and decided the wood
of the frame was at least oak, if not ironwood. The
frame wasn't exactly top-heavy, but without someone
to steady it at the other end, it would easily tip over.
Betsy's shop was cozy, not spacious, and her front door
was of an ordinary size. She hadn't realized there was
so sharp a curve from right inside the door to between
the white dresser and the counter. How was she to get
the long, inflexible frame and its clumsy burden to the
door?

By pulling and shifting and, at one point, climbing
up onto the counter and down the other side to adjust
the angle of the frame.

But the door opened inward, and so the frame had to
be moved backward again. And then the door must be
propped open—no employee had propitiously turned
up, of course—and the struggle begun again.

At last Betsy got the stand most of the way out the
door and was beginning to fear there wasn't enough
sidewalk. She was pausing to consider this new com-
plication when the quilt suddenly slid away, like a giant
snake heading for the underbrush. Betsy grabbed for it,
then saw it was being draped over the arms of Mildred
Feeney, who was smiling at her. "If we take the quilt

off," she said, "the stand folds up and we can carry it to the booth quite easily."

"Oh? Oh, yes, I should have thought of that," said Betsy, blushing at herself for also thinking, even for an instant, that the quilt had made an attempt to escape. Even if the frame didn't fold, which it did (the hinges being clearly visible once the quilt was off), it would have been lighter and easier to manage without all those thick yards of fabric on it.

The naked V, folded, was not hard to manage, especially with Mildred, who was stronger than she looked, helping.

Mildred had already put a cash box and an immense roll of double tickets in the booth. After Betsy helped redrape the quilt, Mildred fixed Betsy with a look. "They're a dollar apiece," she said in her sweet but firm old-woman's voice, "six for five dollars. How many shall I tear off for you?"

Betsy sighed and bought twenty dollars' worth, asking in her own firmest voice for a receipt so she could record the money as a charitable donation. It never occurred to her that she might win—Betsy never won raffles.

Perhaps, she reflected on her way back into the shop, she had been a little too quick to promise her sponsorship of Lars and his Steamer. Between the parts he had had to order—very expensive and one all the way from England—and the strange, also expensive, requirements in cylinder and gear oil and kerosene for the pilot light, and the lousy mileage it got on gasoline—*plus* the entry fee for the Antique Car Run and raffle tickets, this was turning out to be a very expensive sponsorship. She was also beginning to regret that she'd volunteered to help out at the Run. It was taking too much time away from the shop. And since her volunteer assignment on the day of the New London–New Brighton run was to record the names of the drivers as they left on the run, and then to help prepare and serve lunch at the halfway stop, she wasn't even going to get to ride with Lars next Saturday.

She began the opening-up process in her shop. She was going to be in and out today, so Godwin was going to be helped by Shelly Donohue, an elementary school teacher who worked for Betsy during the summer months. Betsy turned on the lights, put the start-up money in the cash register, and tuned the radio to a classical station with the volume barely audible. She was just plugging in the old vacuum cleaner when Shelly came in.

"Did you hear the latest?" asked Shelly breathlessly.

Shelly was an inveterate gossip, and her "latest" was usually exceedingly trivial, but Betsy politely delayed turning on the machine so she could hear whatever the silly tidbit was.

"John threw Godwin out."

Betsy dropped the wand. "Oh, Shelly, are you sure?"

"How sure do you want? Godwin slept at my house last night."

"Is he very upset?"

"We sat up till two this morning, and he never stopped crying for more than five minutes at a time. He's a real mess."

"I suppose that means he won't be in today?" Betsy felt for Godwin, but she really needed two people in the shop on weekends. Especially this weekend, with two attractions bringing lots of visitors to town.

"He said he'd be here, but to tell you he'd be late, because he had to go get his clothes. He got a call from a neighbor that they're in a big pile along the curb outside John's condo."

Betsy sat down. Godwin's clothes were enormously expensive: Armani suits, silk shirts, alpaca sweaters, handmade shoes, all bought by John, of course—Godwin couldn't have bought the sleeve of one suit on the salary Betsy paid him. John loved to ornament his handsome boy toy and had taught Godwin to treat the clothes with respect. If they had been unceremoniously dumped out in the street, this wasn't a mere lover's quarrel; John must be serious about the breakup.

"This is terrible. I feel so sorry for Godwin! And I can't imagine him coming in after having to pick his beautiful clothes up off the ground. How cruel of John!"

"I agree. Goddy is so upset that even if he does turn up, I don't think he'll be much use. So what are we going to do? With you out most of the day, we have to have another person."

"All right, call Caitlin and see if she's available. If she isn't, go down the list. If you get down to Laverne, you'll want a third person." Caitlin, a high school senior, had been stitching since she was six; Laverne, a retired brewery worker, barely knew linen from Aida and was afraid of the cash register. "Meanwhile, I hope he comes before I have to get back out to the booth. I really want to talk to him. Has he got someplace to go? I mean, besides your place?"

"I don't think so. He was crying that John made him give up all his real friends, except me and you. But he can stay with me for as long as he wants. I've got a spare bedroom. And Goddy doesn't mind the dogs."

"Is that what the fight was about, John's jealousy?" asked Betsy.

"Something like that. Goddy says John accused him—falsely, Goddy says—of flirting with Donny DePere at a party. But John is very jealous, he won't let Goddy have any male friends, even straight ones." A smile flickered across Shelly's face. "Goddy says he's so frustrated he caught himself flirting with a girl just to keep his hand in."

"What do you think, was Godwin flirting with another man?"

Shelly hesitated only briefly. "Yes, I think so. But it's still John's fault, don't you think?"

"I don't think I have a right to an opinion. I don't know the rules of that relationship, and I only met John once."

"Yes, well, that snotty attitude you saw at your Christmas party—" Shelly assumed a lofty attitude and sniffed lightly. " 'How terribly tedious your friends are, Goddy,' " she murmured, then grimaced. "That's John all over. What a jerk!"

"Yes, but he's a wealthy jerk. That enables Godwin to work here for very low wages, for which I am very grateful," said Betsy heartlessly. "So encourage Goddy to kiss and make up, will you?"

The door went *Bing!* and they turned to see the subject of their conversation come in. Godwin was a handsome young man of barely medium height, slim and blond, wearing tight jeans, a white linen shirt with no collar, and loafers with no socks. Normally ebullient and witty, he was looking very woebegone at the moment.

"Hi, Godwin," said Betsy. "I was afraid we might

not see you today. I'm so sorry about you and John."

At this show of sympathy, tears formed in his sky-blue eyes. "What am I going to *do*?"

Shelly went to him. "You're going to stay with me until John comes to his senses," she said, taking him by the arm. "He has to learn that you have feelings, too." She led him to the library table in the middle of the room, and pulled a chair out for him. "Now sit down for a minute and pull yourself together."

"Thank you," murmured Godwin.

"Would you like a cup of coffee? Oh! I haven't made the coffee yet! It'll just take a minute. You just sit and wait, and think happy thoughts."

"All right," he said, but instead he made a little display of his grief, dropping his head and sighing, touching the end of his nose, then wiping under each eye, and sighing again.

Betsy said, pulling the vacuum cleaner over by the door, "Are you going to be able to work today?"

Godwin lifted his head. "Oh, I'll get through it somehow. After all, now I really need the money."

"Shelly says you're staying with her, and can stay as long as you like. That will help."

Godwin smiled sadly. "Shelly is the nicest person in the world. It's *so* lovely having someone coo over you and make you little treats and bring hot cocoa to you in bed. Don't you agree?"

Betsy laughed. "Ever since I was a little child with measles."

Godwin straightened. "Why are you so sure I'm feeling too sorry for myself? John has never gone this far before. My beautiful clothes, all dirty and wrinkled!

Does he think I'm going to go crawling back to him after this?"

"If he threw you out, don't you have to wait for an invitation before you go crawling back?"

"Oh," said Godwin, looking disconcerted. "Well, yes, I suppose I do. Well, say, that puts the ball in his court, doesn't it? I don't have to try to think of an excuse to call him, do I? And when he finds out I've got a place to stay, *he'll* be the one getting anxious. Won't he?"

"I sure hope so. But what do I know? What do you think?"

"I think John plays by his own rules," said Godwin, dropping again into gloom.

Shelly came back with a freshly brewed cup of coffee, and Godwin sat sighing over it while Betsy vacuumed and Shelly dusted. Shelly liked to dust; it gave her lots of opportunities to pause and consider a pattern or a new color of wool or floss. She had yet to take home an entire paycheck, spending most of it on things from the shop. Today she picked out a Terrance Nolan butterfly. "I just love his things, but they're really difficult. I saw you have his kingfishers."

Betsy said, "I saw the models at Stitchville USA, and decided to order three kits; they're gorgeous. And I could sell them if I had a model. Would you be willing, Shelly?"

"Not me! His bugs are enough for me; those kingfishers are murder! Maybe you should ask the Turbo Stitcher."

Bitsy Busby had earned that nickname because she could plow through even a large and complex counted pattern in a week or ten days. A chronic insomniac, she sat up most nights watching old movies on cable and stitching. Despite her speed, her patterns were beautifully worked. She was especially fond of linen, particularly coffee-dyed linen. Godwin had once joked that the reason she was an insomniac was because she absorbed caffeine from the yards of fabric that passed through her fingers.

"Well, I'd better go see what's going on out there," said Betsy. "Wish me luck."

"God bless us every one."

4

The temperature had risen ten degrees in the little while Betsy had been gone. Used to the dry heat of southern California, she was disconcerted by how warm seventy-eight humid degrees could be. Her favorite pant suit, cotton khaki with touches of lace, was too much clothing for this weather even with its short sleeves. She could feel it wilting as she walked to the booth.

One of the women was saying to the man, ". . . a '14 Hupmobile, he wants fifteen thousand for it." She had a phone to her ear, but she was talking to the man.

The man replied, "In running condition?"

"He says it is." She shrugged, showing doubt. "I haven't seen it." The phone made a faint sound, and she replied into it, "Yes, standing by."

Betsy said, "Do you mean there really was a car

called a Hupmobile? I've heard that name, but I thought it was a joke."

The man looked at her. "No, it was founded by brothers named Hupp in 1908 and they made cars until 1940. The early ones are collector's items."

The woman said, "It's a Hupmobile on the back of the old ten-dollar bills. Take a look sometime."

"I'll do that," promised Betsy. "Is fifteen thousand dollars a lot of money for a Hupmobile? I mean, I would have thought so a few months ago, until a friend paid seventeen thousand for a Stanley Steamer."

The man said, "Was it Dr. Fine's?"

"How did—" Then Betsy smiled. "Oh, you must have been bidding on it, too."

But he shook his head. "I like rarities, but I wouldn't own a steamer on a bet. It's just that the world of antique cars, especially the crowd that drives them as opposed to just shows them—is very small. I'm Adam Smith, by the way, and this is Lucille Ziegfield, called Ceil." He bent his head sideways toward the woman standing beside him. Still listening to her cell phone, she nodded at Betsy.

"How do you do?" said Betsy. "This is so interesting and exciting! I had no idea there were people who did this. I'm wondering what makes a person decide to get into these old cars. My friend who bought the Stanley is totally focused on the thing, hardly talks about anything else. That's typical of him, but is that typical of antique car owners?"

Ceil, still listening but apparently to dead air, said, "He has just the one?"

"Well, yes."

"Then he's not typical. Most of the people who get

into this hobby wind up with several, sometimes several dozen. It's not a hobby, it's a sickness. My husband owns seven, all Packards. And not all antiques—the latest model he owns is from 1954."

Betsy wasn't sure whether to smile or offer condolences. What would Lars be like with half a dozen Stanleys? "Judging from the time Lars spends working on his one, I don't see where anyone would find the time to build up a collection," Betsy said.

Adam said, "Well, usually one of them is hogging most of the attention. The owner works on it until it's fixed or he can't stand looking at it anymore, and goes on to another."

"A CASITA," nodded Betsy.

" 'Casita'?"

"In needlework, sometimes one project demands all the attention until it turns into a CASITA, you CAn't Stand IT Anymore. So you go on to something else."

Adam nodding, laughed. "Who would have thought antique cars and needlework would have something in common?"

"I never even thought ordinary people could own antique cars," said Betsy. "I mean, I thought they were all in museums. Well, except Jay Leno, I know he owns some. But I certainly didn't know there were clubs of people who drive them."

Ceil said into her phone, "Well, that's politics," folded up her phone, and said to Adam, "The Studebaker the governor was riding in broke down on Selby, so he got out and went home."

"Damn!" muttered Adam, snapping his fingers.

Ceil continued to Betsy, "It's mostly men who get into this. It's not just the money—it takes a working knowledge of machinery, lots of heavy lifting, and a willingness to get really dirty. You'll see some fellow coming out of a shed in the evening with greasy clothes and disgusting fingernails, and only on second look realize he's the richest man in town."

"Who's the richest man in town?" asked a new voice, and Betsy turned to see Joe Mickels standing close behind her, an expression of deep suspicion on his face. A short, bandy-legged man, he had a wide, thin mouth under a great beak of a nose flanked by large white sideburns. He was in, for him, casual summer wear: light blue suit, white canvas shoes, white shirt, light blue necktie. Joe was the richest man in Excelsior, though he didn't want that fact generally known. He had dated Betsy for a short while earlier in the year, and had, in what he considered a tender moment, confided his financial status. Now that the brief romance was over, he constantly suspected her of talking about him, sharing the facts of his wealth with all and sundry.

"I have no idea," replied Betsy coldly. "We were talking about wealthy men who behave like garage mechanics around their antique automobiles."

"How old does a car have to be before it's an antique?" asked Joe.

Adam replied, "Well, for this year's run it's 1912 or earlier."

"Well, then, I've got an antique car."

Betsy had seen Joe's car. It was an immaculate 1969 Lincoln, old but hardly an antique. She frowned at him, and he twinkled at her as if telling her to watch him at work. He said to Adam, "She's seen my Lincoln, but I also have a 1909 McIntyre."

"I didn't know that!" said Betsy.

"There's a lot you don't know about me," said Joe, twinkling more broadly, and continued to Adam, "My grandfather bought it new, then my uncle owned it, then my brother, and now it's mine."

"Does it run?" asked Adam, and Betsy heard a slight change in Adam's voice. Though he was trying to sound casual, it seemed he was very interested in Joe's reply.

"Oh, yes, I started it up last Thursday. It's up on blocks, because it's got these funny big wheels, like wagon wheels, that used to have hard rubber around the rims, but they're worn right down to the metal. But it runs. I cranked her up and ran her for fifteen minutes, then shut her down again. I start her up once a month spring, summer, and fall, run her long enough to circulate the oil and water, then in November I drain the radiator, crankcase, and gas tank, and fill it all up again in the spring, and recharge the battery. That's what my uncle did. I used to help him when I was a boy. I understand some of these old cars are valuable, so I mean to keep her in running order."

"I wish I'd known you had an old car," said Betsy.

"Then I don't see why you didn't ask me," said Joe indifferently, turning a shoulder to her as he focused on Adam. "Of course, I couldn't have taken her for a ride, not without tires, and I don't know where to buy them."

"I could probably give you a source," said Adam. "If you're interested."

"Well, I don't know. The old car's useless, really. I was just keeping her out of sentiment. My Uncle Frank learned to drive with that car, and he used to give me and my cousins rides in it in the summer days of my youth. I think he'd halfway forgotten he had it, and my brother never drove it at all. I found it in an old barn a few years ago and had it moved to a heated shed, because I remembered a magazine article from somewhere that said some of them are valuable to collectors. I don't know if she's of any real value, since she's a McIntyre, and I never heard of that brand, not like the Maxwell, or a Cadillac or a Model T."

"How much of it is original?" asked Adam.

Joe shrugged. "All of it. The engine, chassis, transmission, even the paint job, though it looks a little scabby in places. Original wheels, original seat covers, original glass in the windows. And everything works, except the headlights. My uncle wouldn't drive it at night because the lights were so weak, and now they won't light at all."

"What kind of headlights?"

"Big 'uns, made of brass. There's no lightbulbs in 'em, but I don't know who took 'em out." He scratched an earnest eyebrow to hide the wink he gave Betsy from under his hand.

Adam said, "If they're original, the lights are acetylene, not electric. That kind doesn't use bulbs."

"Acetylene? You mean like a welding torch?"

Adam nodded. "I'd kind of like to see that car."

"Sure, but it's not for sale."

"Who said anything about buying it? I saw one at a show a few years ago, where they asked me to judge. I didn't like the instruments on the dashboard—they were reproductions—and I'd like to see a set of originals."

Joe produced a business card from an inside pocket. "Give me a call sometime. I'll be glad to show it to you." He walked away.

Ceil snorted softly. "Of course you're not interested in a 1909 McIntyre with all original parts!"

Adam shrugged, eyebrows raised in a show of innocence. "Well, now you mention it, I do know a couple of people who might pay good money to buy that car—from me." He looked at the card, pulled out his wallet, and slid it into a pocket.

"If you manage to pry that vehicle out of Joe Mickels's hands for a nickel less than it's worth, you're a better man than most!" she said, laughing.

Betsy decided not to warn Adam after all that Joe's apparently fortuitous appearance at the booth was, in all likelihood, the first move in a plan to sell his McIntyre for at the very least what it was worth. Joe never parted with anything for less than its true value. Moreover, she doubted that sentimental story of it being handed down three generations. Joe? Sentimental? Ha!

There was the sprightly sound of "Für Elise," and Ceil, still smiling, pulled her cell phone from her pocket. "Excelsior," she said into it. "Ah!" She checked her watch. "Thanks!" she added, and disconnected. "The Winton just came onto Minnetonka Boulevard. It should be here in about twenty minutes."

"Not the Stanley?" asked Betsy.

"Why the Stanley?" replied the woman.

"Well, I just thought, because Stanleys are so fast."

The woman laughed. "Yes, for about twenty-five miles. Then they have to stop for water. Every blinking twenty-five miles they have to stop for water. And of course, if they blow a gasket, or the pilot light goes out, or they run out of steam, then the delays really mount up."

Betsy flashed on Lars laughing as he chuffed around

the table in Crewel World, calling "Get a horse!" to imaginary internal combustion cars. Apparently the laugh was not entirely his alone.

She had her clipboard ready when a soft-yellow car with brown fenders came up the street. It didn't look like a car from the teens, but more like something out of an early-thirties movie, with its sleek modeling, long hood, and deeply purring motor. A solidly built, prosperous-looking man in a cream suit was driving, and a very pretty woman wearing a cloche hat sat beside him. They both smiled at Betsy as the car pulled up.

"Number ten," he announced, and Betsy checked off Number Ten, a 1912 Winton, on her list, noting the time beside it.

"Are we the first?" asked the man, though that was obviously the case; there were no other cars in sight.

"Yes, sir, you are," said Betsy. She pointed with her pen at the booth. "Please check in with Adam Smith. He'll tell you where to park."

The Winton had only just moved on down the street when Betsy heard the now-familiar loud and breathy whistle of Lars's Stanley. She looked around and saw it, wreathed in steam, rolling smoothly up Lake toward her. She waited until he pulled up beside her, all smiles, before noting the time. He was one minute, twelve seconds behind the leader.

"Beat 'em all," he announced. "I told you the Stanley was a fast one. I bet number two won't be here for—" He broke off, staring up the street at the Winton pulling up to the curb a little beyond the booth.

"Sorry," said Betsy. But she was smiling.

"Oh, well, like they say, this isn't a race," said Lars, but his smile was now forced.

"How'd she run?" asked Betsy.

"Sweet as milk, and smooth as silk," said Lars. "But I'm thinking I should've looked around for a 1914 model; they have condensers in them, so you don't need to stop every thousand yards to take on water. Someone in St. Paul says he heard there's a guy with one—"

"No, no!" said Betsy. "You don't want to sell this one already! You just got it all restored!"

"Oh, I would never sell this one," Lars replied. "But the 1914, with a condenser . . ." His eyes had gone dreamy. Then he shook himself. "Do I just go up and park behind that yellow car?"

"No, check in at the booth first. Mr. Smith will tell you where to park. And Lars, this time talk to Jill first before you buy another Stanley." But she was talking to his back and he blew his whistle before she'd finished.

There was a half-hour gap before the rest of the cars started trickling in. The trickle grew quickly to a steady stream that as quickly diminished again to a trickle, until Betsy had checked off all but two cars. She was getting very warm standing out in the sun, and suspected her nose was getting sunburned. She wished she'd thought to wear a hat. And sunglasses.

A rust-brown two-seater came up the street, its engine going *diddle-diddle-hick-diddle*. It was a Maxwell with black leather seats and black trim, the top half of its windshield folded down. The car's wax finish shimmered in the bright sunlight as the engine idled unevenly.

The couple driving the car had also dressed in period costumes, he in a big off-white coat called a "duster," a pinch-brim hat in a tiny, dark-check pattern. Goggles with thick rubber edges covered his eyes. There was a dab of grease on his cheek. She wore a duster with leg-o'-mutton sleeves, a huge hat swathed in veils, and sunglasses.

"We're number twenty, the Birminghams, Bill and Charlotte," said the woman, who was on Betsy's side of the car—like most of these antiques, the steering wheel was on the right. The man stared straight ahead, his gauntleted hands tightly gripping the wheel.

"How long do we have here before we start back?" asked Charlotte, pushing aside her veil so she could wipe her face with a handkerchief. Her face looked pale as well as sweaty—and no wonder, thought Betsy, swathed in fabric like that.

"They're asking the drivers to stay at least an hour," replied Betsy. "And just so you know, there's a reporter from the *Excelsior Bay Times* here, asking to interview some of you."

The driver shook his head and grunted, "No."

The woman apologized. "He's feeling cranky. Something's wrong with the engine, we had trouble the whole trip. He needs to tinker with it, or we'll never make the return. I'm going to get out here," she said to him. "I've got to shed a layer or two or I'll just die. Where do we park?" she asked Betsy.

"First you have to check in—up there, at the booth. Adam Smith will tell you where to park."

The woman hesitated, then sighed. "Oh, all right, I'll ride up with you," she said, replying to an unvoiced complaint from Bill. Betsy smiled. Amusing how people who had been married for a long time could do things like that.

The woman resettled herself, and the little car went

diddle-hick-diddle up the street to the white booth.

The last car in, a red-orange model, was small and light. It was a real horseless carriage, looking far more like a frail little buggy than a car. It had no hood, just a low dashboard that curved back toward the driver's shins. He was a slim young man in a tight-fitting cream-colored suit, a high-collared white shirt with a small black bow tie, and a straw boater atop his dark auburn hair. He wasn't behind a steering wheel, but had one hand on a "tiller," a curved silver pipe that ran up from under the dash. The dust-white wheels of his automobile were the right size for bicycles, with wire spokes. The vehicle came to a trembling halt beside Betsy, whose mouth was open in delight. Here, in person, was the car embroidered in the center of Mildred Feeney's quilt, the car that was the very symbol of the Antique Car Club. Before she could check her list to see who was driving it, the driver smiled and said, "Owen Carpenter. Driving a 1902 Oldsmobile, single cylinder."

Betsy made a checkmark beside Number Seven on her list, and wrote the time. She directed him to Adam Smith at the booth and stayed in place a minute to watch the Olds toddle down the street. Its little engine, located somewhere on the underside, sounded a very authoritative "Bap!" at brief intervals.

Then, her work done, Betsy walked slowly to the booth and past it, looking from side to side at the veterans. That Oldsmobile she had just checked in was the oldest in today's run, having survived its first century, but by definition all the cars here were pioneers, and the oldest ones looked like the buggies and wagons they shared the roads with when they were young. Some had names anyone would recognize: Ford, Oldsmobile,

Cadillac. Some were unfamiliar: Everett, Schacht, Brush. Most were brightly painted, orange, yellow, red, blue, brown, green, but some wore basic black. All were surprisingly tall, with a running board to step up on, then another step up to the seats, which themselves were more like upholstered chairs or sofas than modern car seats. They all had brass trim and most featured alertly upright windshields. All but the Olds had wooden spokes on their wheels.

Two men were poking under the hoods and one was on his back doing something to the undercarriage, paying tribute to the experimental nature of these engines and drive mechanisms, but the rest stood in gleaming perfection while people gathered to ask questions or take pictures. The Stanley was leaking steam from several sources, but Lars seemed unconcerned and was boasting to a trio of young men about his trip. He had a bad scald on the back of one hand.

Betsy shook her head, at him and at all the drivers. Seeing these old, *old* cars, and knowing they'd been driven here from St. Paul, was like finding that your great-grandfather was not only still around, but decked out in white flannel trousers and using a wooden racket, capable of the occasional game of tennis.

She gave the clipboard to Adam and went to see how things were going in Crewel World.

It was a huge relief to step out of the glare into the air-conditioned interior. Even better, there were a fair number of customers—a few, by their costumes, from the antique car group.

Godwin wasn't in sight. Betsy raised an inquiring eyebrow at Shelly, who pointed with a sideways nod of her head toward the back of the shop. Betsy went into the little storeroom and heard the sound of weeping coming from the small rest room off it. She tapped lightly on the door. "Godwin?" she called.

"Oh, go away!"

"Why don't you go home?"

"Because I haven't got a home."

"How long have you been in there?"

"I don't know."

"Well, you're not doing us any good holed up like this."

"I won't ask you to pay me for the time."

"Oh, for goodness' sake, Godwin, that's not what I mean! Go over to Shelly's house, you idiot!"

"I know what you mean. I just wish—"

"What do you wish?"

"I wish I could stop feeling sorry for myself."

"Here's an idea. Come out of there and take a walk down Lake Street. You should see these wonderful old cars! They are so beautiful and exotic, just the sort of thing you'd love. And some of the people who ride in them are in period dress." Godwin loved costume parties.

But he only said, "Uh-huh," in a very disinterested voice.

"All right, then go down to the art fair. See if you can find Irene." Irene Potter was sitting with Mark Duggan of Excelsior's Water Street Gallery. Irene's blizzard piece was supposed to be prominently featured, its price a breathtaking six thousand dollars. It was not expected to sell; this was Mr. Duggan's way of introducing the art world to Irene. Irene had done several more pieces and been written up in the *Excelsior Bay Times*, and was behaving badly about being "discovered."

"It's too hot to be walking around in the sun," said Godwin pettishly, though he'd been telling everyone that he was the first to see her potential as a Serious Artist.

"Well, then how about I take you and Shelly out to dinner tonight? It'll probably be late, I don't know how long I'll be in St. Paul, but if you can wait, I'll take you anywhere you want to go."

There was the sound of a nose being blown. "Well," said Godwin in a voice not *quite* so disinterested, "how about Ichiban's, that Japanese restaurant where they juggle choppers and cook your shrimp right in front of you?"

"Fine, if we can get in without a reservation. Because I really don't know what time I'll be back."

"We can call from Shelly's before we leave," suggested Godwin, giving up his struggle to sound sad.

"Fine." Betsy went back out into the shop. Shelly was talking to a man trying to pick something for a birthday present. "All I know is, she pulls the cloth tight in a round wooden thing, and then sews all over it," he was saying. And Caitlin was helping a woman put together the wools she needed for a needlepoint Christmas stocking.

A woman in an ankle-length white cotton dress trimmed in heavy lace was looking around and not finding whatever she was wanting. "May I help you?" asked Betsy.

The woman turned. "Oh, hello again!" She smiled at Betsy's blank face and said, "You clocked us in just a few minutes ago. The 1910 Maxwell? I was wearing a big hat?"

"Oh!" said Betsy. "Yes, now I remember you! Wow,

you went costumed all the way, didn't you? First that big coat and hat, now this wonderful dress! Who do you get to make them for you?"

"The coat is a replica, but this dress and the hat are originals." She did a professional model's turn.

"They *are*?"

"Oh, yes. I collect antique clothes. I like to wear them, so it keeps me on my diet." She laughed and brushed at the tiny bits of floss clinging to her skirts. "I'm also a stitcher, as you can see. Do you know if this store has the Santa of the Forest?"

"We did, but I sold the last one yesterday. I've got more on order, but they won't come in for a week or two, probably."

" 'We'? You work here?"

"Yes, ma'am. In fact, this is my shop. I'm Betsy Devonshire."

"Well, how do you do? I'm Charlotte Birmingham. I'd be out there helping Bill with the Maxwell, but I don't know one end of a wrench from another. I see you have knitting yarns as well. I used to knit, but that was a long time ago. Things have changed a great deal since my time." She shook her head as she glanced around at the baskets of knitting yarn. "Back in my teens, there was embroidery floss and there was wool for crewel, and wool or acrylic for knitting." She picked up a skein of silver-gray yarn of grossly varying thickness. "This is different. But what on earth can you make with it?"

"Look up there," said Betsy, gesturing at a shawl suspended on strings from the ceiling. She had nearly broken her neck fastening that up there.

"Why, it's lovely!" Charlotte exclaimed, and it was, all delicate open work, the uneven yarn making it look

as if it were knit from fog. She reached up to feel the
edge between a thumb and forefinger. "Oooooh, soft!"

"It's surprisingly easy to work with," said Betsy, who
had also knit the shawl.

"Really?" said Charlotte. Then she glanced at the
price tag on the yarn and hastily put it back in the basket. "Actually, I came in for some DMC 285. It's a
metallic, silver. I couldn't find it at Michael's."

"My counted cross stitch materials are in the back.
Come with me, I'll show you." The back third of
Betsy's shop was devoted solely to counted. It was set
off from the front by a ceiling-high pair of box shelves.
Charlotte went to a tall spinner rack of DMC floss, but
Betsy said, "No, that metallic comes on a spool. Over
here."

A small rack in one of the "boxes" held spools of
metallic floss. "Here it is," said Betsy.

"Thank you. So long as we're back here, do you have
cashel?"

"Certainly. What color are you looking for?" Betsy
didn't have the enormous selection of fabric that Stitchville USA had, but she was proud to have a wide selection, rather than restricting her shop to Aida and
linen.

A while later, Betsy rang up a substantial sale—
Charlotte was like many stitchers. She couldn't resist
poking through the patterns and the rack of stitching
accessories, and adding to her initial purchase.

And then, riffling the sale basket of painted needlepoint canvases next to the cash register, Charlotte found
a painted canvas of a gray hen that would look "darling" made into a tea cozy, so then Betsy had to help
her select the gray, taupe, white, yellow, and red yarns

needed to complete the pattern. She added the customary free needle and needle threader to the bag.

"Are you from around here?" asked Betsy after Charlotte had paid for her additional selections. "We have a group that meets every Monday afternoon in the shop to stitch. They do all kinds of needlework so you can bring whatever you're working on."

"Oh, that sounds nice," said Charlotte wistfully. "But we live in Roseville, clear the other side of the Cities, which makes an awfully long drive."

Reminded, Betsy checked her watch and made an exclamation. "We'd better get back out there. It's almost time to start back to St. Paul."

Charlotte said, "I'm not going to ride back in the Maxwell. It's too hot, and the jiggle was making me sick."

" 'Jiggle'?"

"It's a two-cylinder and it jiggles all the time. Especially when it's not running well. After a while you begin to think your stomach will never be right again."

"Then how are you going to get home?"

"Oh, I'll ask Ceil or Adam or Nancy if I can ride with them to St. Paul. I can help out in the booth until Bill gets back. Then I'll help him put the Max into the trailer for the trip home."

"Well, I'm supposed to go over there, too. Would you care to ride with me?" After all, Charlotte, who had come in looking for a two-dollar item, had just spent nearly seventy dollars.

"Why, thank you, I'd like that very much. Let me go tell Bill."

They went out together and up the sidewalk to the brown car with a man leaning over the engine revealed by a rooked-up hood. He, too, had removed his duster, and had wrapped a towel around his waist to protect his immaculate white flannel trousers from the grease he was getting on his hands and on his fine linen shirt. Another towel, liberally smeared with grease, was draped over a fender. His head was well under the hood and he was muttering under his breath.

Charlotte came up behind him and said, "Bill, I'm riding to St. Paul with Betsy Devonshire here, one of the volunteers. All right?"

"Okay," grunted Bill. Metal clanged on metal. "Ow."

She bent over to murmur something to him, laughed softly at his unheard reply, touched him lightly on the top of his rump. "See you later," she concluded, and went to open the passenger side door and haul out in one big armload a carpet bag with wooden handles, the duster she'd been wearing, and the big, well-wrapped hat.

"Let's go see if Adam will keep these in the booth for me," she said. "And maybe he has something for me to do."

Adam sighed over the size of Charlotte's bundle, but found a corner for it. And he didn't have anything for her to do, not at the moment. "But say, if you want to assist Betsy in recording the departure times, that would be nice. They are supposed to tie their banners on the left side, but some interpret that to mean the driver's side, and if their steering wheel is on the right, they put it there; and some don't read the instructions at all and put it on the back end or forget to put it on at all."

Betsy said, "That's right. I had to ask a lot of the drivers what their entry number was because it wasn't where I could see it when they drove up." One had had to get out of his car and dig it out of the wicker basket that served as a trunk, remarking he didn't think it mattered until the actual run.

"If you'll stand so the cars run between you," said Adam, "one of you is bound to see the number."

Betsy, remembering the wicker basket, asked, "Why *does* it matter? If it's not a race, and they don't get a medallion for finishing this run, who cares what time they leave here?"

"We need to keep track," replied Adam. "So if someone doesn't show up at the other end, we know to go looking for him."

Ceil said, "They have special trucks that follow the route between New London and New Brighton, but they're not here today. Someone could break down, and if we weren't keeping track, they might not be missed until dark. Most of these cars shouldn't be driven after dark."

Betsy nodded. "I see."

Ceil checked her watch. "The first arrivals can start back in about fifteen minutes. That will be the Winton and the Stanley."

Betsy said, "Not the Steamer."

Ceil asked, "Why not?"

"He lives here, he just wanted to see if the car could make it from St. Paul. Kind of a tryout for the big run."

Adam asked, "His is the Steamer coming to the run, isn't it?"

Betsy nodded, then said, "I haven't seen the whole list of people signed up. Is there only one Steamer?"

Adam nodded. "Yes. Generally we get only one. The steam people have their own clubs. Their requirements and rules are different. Here, why don't you sit inside the booth? It's shade at least."

"Thanks." Betsy and Charlotte came in. The booth was roomy enough, even with the big quilt on its stand taking up most of the center. The booth had a board running around three sides of it that made a counter. Handouts about the Antique Car Club of Minnesota made stacks along it. There were also a few maps of the route stapled to a three-page turn-by-turn printed guide, for drivers who had lost or mislaid theirs. Postcards featuring pictures of antique cars were for sale. Mildred had taken up a post, her cash box on one side and the immense roll of double raffle tickets on the other. By the number of tickets dropped into a big, clear plastic jug, business had not been brisk, but she professed herself satisfied.

"Here, sit beside me," she said to Betsy. "And you, too, of course," she added to Charlotte.

Charlotte sat on Mildred's other side. She picked up a corner of the quilt and said, "Oh, it's embroidery, not appliqué. That's so much more work, isn't it? How many of you worked on that quilt?"

"It varies from year to year. Five of us did it this year. We start right after each run to work on next year's. I hope you noticed that every car on it is a car that has actually been on the run. When we started out, we didn't know much about antique cars. We got a book from the library and made photocopies of cars that we were interested in, and Mabel turned them into transfer patterns and put them on the squares, and we stitched them. The center square is always the emblem of the club—the Merry Oldsmobile."

Betsy said, "Oh, like from the song,

> *'Come away with me, Lucille,*
> *in my merry Oldsmobile'?"*

"Yes, that's the one," said Mildred, with a little smile. "Though I think the theme of the run should be 'Get Out and Get Under.' You know," she started to sing in a cracked soprano,

> " *'A dozen times they'd start to hug and kiss,*
> *and then the darned old engine, it would miss,*
> *and then he'd have to get under,*
> *get out and get under,*
> *and fix up his automobile!'* "

Betsy said, "I remember my grandmother singing that song!" She looked up the street. "Looks as if things haven't changed much with those old machines." The driver who'd been under his car earlier was still under it.

Adam put in, "That's why the run isn't a race. Just getting across the finish line is enough of a challenge, and anyone who makes it has earned his medallion. By the way," he added, holding out a clipboard, "here comes the Winton."

"Oops!" said Betsy, grabbing it. "Come on, Charlotte, time to get to work!"

The cars were spaced about three minutes apart—except when, as sometimes happened, a driver couldn't get his started, and there was a wider gap while another car was waved into its place. This happened with Bill Birmingham's Maxwell. A thin crowd stood on the sidewalks to cheer and clap as the gallant old veterans putt-putted, or whicky-daddled, or pop-humbled their

way out of town. Bill finally got his Maxwell started
after all the others had left. Charlotte blew kisses at the
car, which despite Bill's efforts still went *diddle-diddle-
hick-diddle* down the road. "Happy trails, darling!" she
called, then turned to Betsy. "Whew, am I glad I'm not
going on that ride!"

5

Betsy checked on Crewel World one last time before leaving for St. Paul. Godwin seemed to have come out of his funk, and was assisting a customer trying out a stitch under the Dazor light. Betsy caught his eye and told him she'd try to be back before closing.

Then it was through the back into the potholed parking lot with Charlotte to Betsy's car.

Betsy's old Tracer had never recovered from a winter incident involving sliding off a snow-covered road into a tree. In seeking a replacement, she considered several high-quality used cars, envied the mayor his amusing cranberry-red Chrysler PT, but had at last bought a new, deep blue Buick Century four-door, fully loaded. It was the nicest new car she'd ever owned and she was very proud of it.

But Charlotte was obviously used to a better variety

of cars. She simply laid her duster and big hat in the back seat with her stitchery bag, hiked the bottom of her antique white dress halfway up her shins, and climbed in the front passenger seat.

They took 7 to 494, up it to 394, then skirted downtown Minneapolis on 94 to St. Paul, taking the Capitol exit.

Crossing over the freeway put them on a street leading to a big white building modeled on the U.S. Capitol—except the Minnesota version had a very large golden chariot pulled by four golden horses on top of the portico. There were cars parked in slots in front of the capitol, but no people standing around.

Betsy said, "Looks as if we beat everyone. Even the booth is empty." A twin to the booth in Excelsior stood on the wide street at the foot of the capitol steps. They drove around back and found a parking space. After the air-conditioned interior of Betsy's car, the moist heat was again almost insufferable. Nevertheless, Charlotte donned her hat, draping the veils carefully around her head and shoulders—"It's easier than trying to carry it," she remarked. She did carry her duster and a handful of pamphlets she'd scooped out of the booth in Excelsior. Betsy brought her and Charlotte's stitching. She noticed that by the worn appearance of Charlotte's carpet bag, it was another antique. Its nubby surface was scattered with "orts," what stitchers called the little ends of floss. They walked around the blinding white building and across the broad paved area to the booth, where they collapsed on folding chairs.

"Whew!" said Betsy, fanning herself with a pamphlet. "How did people stand this back before air-conditioning?"

"It's not so hard to bear if you don't keep going in and out of air-conditioned spaces. People survived much worse weather than this before there was air-conditioning. Think of St. Louis—or Savannah—back when what I'm wearing was a marvelous improvement on the much heavier Civil War era clothing."

"Yes, of course, you're right. You know, we didn't have air-conditioning until I was about fourteen, and while I remember how much I loved having it, I don't remember suffering like I am now without it." She looked out across the shimmering heat lake of the parking area to the trees lifting tired arms in the sun. "Hard to believe we had our last snow just two months ago."

"And that in three months we may have another one," said Charlotte. "But that's why we love it here in Minnesota." Her tone was only a little dry. She reached into her carpet bag and pulled out a square of linen tacked onto a wooden frame. On it, in a variety of stitches, was a flowering plant with caterpillars on the leaves and two kinds of bees and a ladybug hovering among the flowers. She saw Betsy's eye on her work and said, "It's from a hanging designed by Grace Christie back in 1909. I'm going to work more of the squares and have them made into pillows."

Betsy said, "Do you know what that plant is? It looks familiar, somehow."

"Someone told me it's borage, an old medicinal herb."

"Oh, of course, 'Borage for Melancholy.' "

Charlotte looked at the nearly finished piece. "Does it work, I wonder?"

"I understand St. John's Wort does. So perhaps borage does, too."

Two tourists in shorts and sunglasses—a man and a woman—came up. Pointing, the woman said, "What a crazy hat!"

Charlotte laughed and said, "You're too kind."

The man said, "We came to see the old cars."

"They're on a round trip to Excelsior," said Charlotte.

"Who drove to Excelsior?" asked the woman, frowning.

"The owners of the antique cars," replied Charlotte.

"So where are the cars?" asked the man.

"The owners drove them to Excelsior." An element of patience had come into Charlotte's voice.

"Why did they do that? The paper said they were going to be here."

"They were here," said Charlotte more patiently. "But they drove to Excelsior to put on a display there."

"But I thought the paper said they'd be on display here!" said the woman.

"They were here, early this morning," said Charlotte, speaking very slowly now. "Then they drove to Excelsior. And now they've started driving back. At"—she consulted her watch—"four-thirty or so, they should be back from Excelsior."

"How come they're driving from Excelsior?" said the man. "The paper said they'd be here."

Betsy started to make a low humming noise, and when the woman looked at her, she coughed noisily, eyes brimming.

"They *were* here," said Charlotte, ignoring Betsy, "and they'll be back here in a couple of hours."

"I don't understand why they aren't here now, when the paper said they would be," said the woman.

Charlotte, speaking as if to a first grader, said, "The paper said they'd be here early this morning, then that they'd be driving from here to Excelsior, then that they'd return here to be on display again."

"Oh," said the woman, looking curiously at Betsy, who, hands cupped over nose and mouth, was trying unsuccessfully to contain that cough. "Thank you. Come on, Lew," she added, taking the man by the arm and leading him away. "I don't remember reading all that stuff about them being here and not being here and being here again."

As they trailed out of sight, Betsy could at last release the laughter. "Why didn't you just give those two a map and suggest they go meet the cars en route?" she asked.

"And have them run someone into a ditch?" retorted Charlotte.

"Never fear," said Betsy. "Those two couldn't possibly follow that map. They would have ended up back across the border in the place of their birth: Iowa."

"A distinct improvement to the gene pool in both places," said Charlotte in a dead-on Hepburn drawl.

Betsy laughed some more and Charlotte joined in. Insulting Iowa is a peculiar Minnesota custom—and while Iowans are happy to reciprocate, their jokes aren't considered half as clever. In Minnesota, anyway.

A woman drove by in a Land Rover, slowing to wave from inside the vehicle at Betsy and Charlotte. Betsy recognized Ceil, one of the women in the Excelsior booth. The Rover went on around to the parking lot in back of the Capitol building.

She came back on foot to say, "What, Adam isn't here yet?"

"Not yet," said Betsy and turned to greet another pair of tourists.

"My uncle once told me his grandfather owned a 1914 Model T Ford," said the man. "But we were here before the cars left on their run, and there was a 1910 Ford the driver said was a Model T. Who was right?"

"I—I don't know," said Betsy, and listened for Charlotte's cough.

Which kindly didn't come. Instead, she stood and said, "The first Model T appeared in 1908, and wasn't replaced by the Model A until around 1928. Of course, Henry Ford made constant changes and improvements as the years went by, but it was always called the Model T."

"Why Model T?" asked the woman.

Ceil came over to join the conversation, "Well, every time he reinvented his car, he gave the model the next letter of the alphabet. By the time Tin Lizzie came along, he was up to T. I don't know why he stuck to T so long; the 1912 model was very different from the 1908 one, and the 1927 Model T was a very different car again. The car that replaced it was the more expensive and sophisticated Model A, which is apparently why he decided to start over."

The couple asked a few more questions, took a brochure on the Antique Car Club, and drifted away. Betsy said, "I didn't know any of that!"

Charlotte smiled. "I only cling to my ignorance when it comes to actually working on restoration and repairs. I prefer to let Bill pack the wheels or replace the transmission bands." She held out her slender, long-fingered, and very clean hands, regarding them complacently.

"Be glad Bill didn't get a Stanley Steamer," said

Betsy, "or dirt might not be the worst that can happen. My friend Lars has one, and the places on him that aren't dirty are blistered."

Ceil laughed. "Has he still got both his eyebrows?"

"Well, he has now, since the right one grew back." She sat down beside Charlotte and resumed stitching. Betsy was working on a counted cross stitch pattern worked on black fabric. It had pale green cats' eyes and the merest hint of paws. In crooked lettering down one side it said, *Sure Dark in Here, Isn't It?* Betsy was adding whiskers in back stitching, counting carefully to make sure they were placed properly.

"Where are you going to hang that?" asked Charlotte.

"Six, seven, eight—in my bathroom," replied Betsy. "The thread glows in the dark."

"Hang it next to the light switch," advised Charlotte. "I'd hate to try to find the . . . er, by the light that thing will give off."

Ceil giggled.

"I don't see Mildred," said Betsy. "Perhaps I should have volunteered to bring the quilt, too."

Charlotte said, "But it wouldn't be any good unless you could sell raffle tickets for it, and Mildred won't let anyone take custody of that roll of tickets or the money jar. That's a job she's very jealous of."

"Speak of the devil," said Ceil, and they looked up to see Mildred, driving a large old Chrysler, pull up beside the booth. She put her car in park, got out, and opened the passenger door. The big heap of quilt engulfed her as she tried to get it out without letting it touch the ground. Betsy and Charlotte hurried to help. The frame was in the back seat, and Betsy wondered how she'd gotten it in there; even with their help, it was a struggle to get it out again. But Mildred again proved stronger than she looked, and was experienced in handling the thing. Under her crisp directions, she and Charlotte set it up in the booth and helped Mildred drape the quilt over it.

Mildred said, "Thank you, Betsy. Now, I'll be right back," and went to park. When she came back, she had the money jar and the big roll of raffle tickets in her arms. Evidently Mildred had hidden them in the trunk.

About twenty minutes later, Ceil said, "Look, here comes Adam at last." Betsy hadn't noticed him drive in, but he was walking from behind the Capitol building, where they—and apparently Adam—had parked.

"What kept you?" demanded Ceil.

"There's an accident in the tunnel," said Adam, meaning a long, curved underpass on 94 in Minneapolis. "It's down to one very slow lane in the eastbound side." He held up a large paper sack. "Plus I stopped for sandwiches." He handed them around.

He'd barely finished his tuna on a whole wheat bun before the first antique car came up, a 1909 Cadillac. Betsy grabbed the board Adam quickly held out, and Charlotte again helped Betsy clock the cars in.

As before, the 1902 Oldsmobile was last—except for Charlotte and Bill's Maxwell.

"Did you see Number Twenty, a rust-brown Maxwell, along the road?" Charlotte asked the driver of the Olds.

"No, when I left Bill was still trying to get it started. And it never caught up with me." Betsy thanked him and waved him through.

"Well, this is a fine thing!" grumbled Charlotte. "I

wonder where he broke down?" She went to talk to Adam, Betsy trailing behind her.

"He was having trouble with it, remember?" she said.

"Yes, but he just waved me off when I went to ask him if he wanted to cancel his return trip," replied Adam. "And it seemed to be running only as ragged as it was when he came into Excelsior."

"I know, I know. That darned machine—and he *would* insist on driving it even though he has other cars that don't misbehave!"

Betsy turned to Ceil and Adam. "Didn't you mention a truck that follows the route looking for breakdowns?"

"No follow-up truck for this run," said Adam.

"Anyway," Ceil said, "doesn't Bill have a cell phone?"

"Yes, he does," said Charlotte, frowning. She went to her old-fashioned carpet bag and rummaged in it for her own very modern cell phone. She turned it on and punched in some numbers.

"That's funny," she said a minute later, the frown a little deeper. "He's not answering."

"Maybe he's gone to find someone to help get his car started," said Betsy.

"Wouldn't matter," Charlotte replied. "He carries that thing with him in his pocket." She dialed the number again, listened awhile, and shut her phone off.

Betsy turned to Adam. "Where is that other woman who was with you in the booth in Excelsior?"

"Nancy's gone home, she could only volunteer this morning. Why?"

"I was thinking, if she's still in Excelsior, we could ask her to follow the route the antique cars took, and see if she can find Bill along the way. But I guess not."

"Still," said Adam, "the next step is to go looking along the route. I'm in charge, I'll go." He reached for a map of the route and left the booth.

Ceil called after him, "Let us know right away when you find him!" She turned to Charlotte. "Can you drive the trailer out to pick him up, or are we going to have to find you a driver?"

Charlotte said, "I don't like to, but I can drive it. What I don't understand is why he didn't call me when he broke down, to tell me what was happening, and where he was. I hope he made it most of the way, then Adam won't have so far to drive."

Charlotte seemed more annoyed than angry at this development, but when she came back to sit with her needlework, she didn't pull the needle out to begin. Betsy was moved to ask, "Are you all right?"

"Yes, of course," said Charlotte. After a bit she said, "Only I can't understand why he didn't call."

"Perhaps the battery in his phone has run down," suggested Betsy.

"Yes, that could be the problem. He's forgotten in the past to shut it off after he's used it." She did pick up her needle then, and put a few stitches in the honeybee's wing then said, as if continuing a conversation she'd been having internally, "Well, it just isn't fair!"

"What isn't fair?"

"What?" said Charlotte, staring at Betsy.

"You said it just isn't fair," said Betsy. "What isn't fair?"

"Oh—nothing. I mean, I didn't mean to say it out loud. I'm just a little upset, that's all. I mean, it isn't like Bill to just sit in his broken-down car, when he has a perfectly good cell phone. And even if you're right, and the battery's gone dead, there's always a gas station or even a house he can go to and use their phone. He promised to be better about this sort of thing, not to leave me sitting and worrying. That's why we got the phones, after all."

"Husbands can be the limit, can't they?"

"Beyond the limit." Then Charlotte smoothed the frown from her forehead with what seemed deliberation and said, "But I don't believe he's neglecting me on purpose. I'm sure as anything that he's underneath the hood trying to fix the engine, and has gotten so involved he's forgotten all about the time and that I'm sitting here, tired and dusty and wanting to go home."

Betsy, remembering how he didn't even come out from under to say goodbye back in Excelsior, said, "Whereas we stitchers never get so involved with our needlework that we forget to fix dinner or pick the kids up after soccer or take the cat to the vet."

The frown that had reclenched Charlotte's face relaxed again, and her eyes twinkled. "Well . . . yes," she admitted. "And Bill has been a lot better lately. When he announced his retirement two years ago, I thought we could travel or take up a hobby we'd both be interested in or at least spend more time together. But he didn't quite give up control at the office, and when he wasn't there, he was working on his car collection. We had a couple of serious fights, and at last I went to a therapist—alone, because Bill wouldn't go, of course—but Dr. Halpern helped me start some serious conversations with Bill, and things have been better lately."

"How many cars does Bill have?" asked Betsy.

"Six, all Maxwells but one. I thought it would be fun, riding down the road in these old cars, going to meets and all. And it is. But there are the hours Bill spends in the shed restoring them, and the hours on the Internet talking with other car nuts, and the days he spends traveling all over the country buying parts."

"He should take you along—I thought you said you wanted to travel."

"But he finds these parts in some very out-of-the-way places, never Barbados or San Francisco or London. And since I don't know what the parts are for, I can't help him shop for them, so I have to go off by myself to whatever museum there is or shop for antique clothing. Sometimes I just go to a movie, which I could do just as well at home." Her voice had become so querulous that she became aware of it, so she shut up and with a sigh tucked her needle into the margin of the fabric. "Oh, I admit it's not all his fault. The therapist advised me to change my own ways a bit, too. And when I did, Bill saw I was serious. He said if I was willing to change, then he started to think maybe he could change a little, too. We've been reconnecting— that's my therapist's term, reconnecting—and things have gotten much better. It will take a while to undo old habits, as we've seen today, but Rome wasn't torn down in a day either, I suppose."

"No," agreed Betsy with a smile.

People came up with questions or to pick up a brochure, but in few enough numbers that Ceil could handle most of them. People were far more interested in talking with the owners of the cars than the people sitting in the booth. They went from car to car with their questions, taking lots of photographs. Now and again there was the sound of an old-fashioned horn going *Ahooooo-ga!*—always accompanied by titters and giggles and a little rush of people heading for the source of the sound, a beautiful 1911 Marmon.

It was nearly an hour later that Ceil's cell phone began to play "Für Elise" and she pulled it from a pocket. "St. Paul," she said into it. "Yes?" She glanced at Charlotte. "Oh. Oh, my," she said and quickly turned her back, going as far away as she could without leaving the booth.

Charlotte and Betsy looked at one another, Betsy with concern, Charlotte with the beginnings of fright. Betsy put a hand on Charlotte's.

"I'm sure it's nothing too serious," said Mildred. "He probably ran off the road, broke an axle or something." That she offered this disaster as "nothing too serious" showed how terribly bad she was thinking it might be, too.

Charlotte began putting her stitchery away, making a fuss about it, keeping herself busy while they waited.

"Char?" said Ceil a few minutes later, and Charlotte turned in her chair. Ceil was looking helpless, as if she couldn't think where to begin.

"What is it, tell me what's wrong!" demanded Charlotte.

"It's Bill. Oh, sweetie, I'm so very sorry—" She sobbed twice, but then took hold of herself and said rapidly, "He's dead, Charlotte. When Adam got there, the fire department was already there, the car was on fire, and Bill was underneath it. That's all they know right now."

Charlotte stared speechless at Ceil. She turned wide, horrified eyes on Betsy, then on Mildred. "No," she said very quietly, and fainted.

6

Adam Smith waited in sick silence as the methodical examination of the scene went on. If someone asked him to list the places on earth he wanted to be, this would be at the bottom or near it. But he couldn't leave. He'd been asked by a police officer to stay. The man had been polite, putting it in the form of a request, but Adam felt it would be put in stronger terms if he refused.

Besides, if he did leave, he'd have to go back to St. Paul, where Charlotte Birmingham waited. And on that list of places to be, going to talk to Charlotte was probably tied for whatever near-bottom place staying here occupied.

Sooner or later they'd let him go, but he had no idea what he could possibly say to Charlotte about what he'd found while driving up County Highway 5.

It was a charming enough section of Minnetonka, a gently hilly area with small, neat cottages on broad lots lining the two-lane road. Just here, there was a white gravel lay-by across the road from a big church, just up from a cemetery. A horribly appropriate location, because here in the lay-by he had found firemen and their truck, and an ambulance, and several squad cars.

And the Maxwell, blackened and blistered.

And Bill, poor dead Bill, lying on the gravel where he'd been dragged out from under the car.

They hadn't covered Bill's body, and Adam's eyes kept wandering to it, sickening him all over again. Medics were standing around him, but in the idle poses that said they had nothing to do, that Bill was far, far beyond anything they could do.

Adam lifted his eyes a little, to watch a uniformed policeman talking to one of the medics and taking notes as he listened to a reply.

The policeman gestured at Bill's body, drawing Adam's attention back to it, so he quickly turned his head to look at Bill's car. There wasn't a crumpled fender, a smashed headlight, even a dent, so there hadn't been an accident. The Maxwell hadn't run into anything, or been run into, or rolled over. It had been driven into this lay-by, which was perhaps an alternate parking lot for the church, now that Adam thought about it. The Maxwell was at the back of the graveled area, shaded by trees. Bill had probably pulled in here when the engine trouble that had plagued him all day got so bad he couldn't continue the run. And Bill had slid under it to check something—no, fix something, because there were tools half-visible in the big puddle of dirty water that surrounded the car. The firemen had made that puddle, putting out the fire that had started while Bill was under it.

The car must have exploded into flame, because if it had been just an ordinary fire, Bill would have rolled out from under. And he hadn't, he'd still been under it when the firemen arrived.

Interesting how Bill's upper legs in their white flannel trousers were only a trifle smoky, his lower ones were untouched, and his brown leather shoes were unmarked by anything but a little dust. While the rest of him was so bad . . . *Why can't they cover him decently?* Adam thought again, yanking his eyes away to watch a policewoman on the other end of the lay-by tying yellow plastic ribbon to a tree, pulling a length from a large roll, then walking to a wooden lamppost out near the road, letting the tape unreel on her wrist. Adam frowned at that, then looked at Bill's Maxwell again. *Crime scene tape? Why?* Despite himself, his attention wandered back to Bill, but ricocheted instantly to the burned-out Maxwell.

There was the crime. What had happened to the car was a sorry crime. Despite its lack of dents, the old machine was history, its metal chassis blistered and blackened, the seats and dash and steering wheel all gone into a heap of ash and metal. Leaves on the branches that overhung the car—it was back here because Bill had sought shade, obviously—were withered or burned away, indicating this had been a serious fire. A great fire could be built from an antique car's interior of varnished wood, leather, and straw stuffing, Adam knew.

The fire truck's engine started up. Adam watched it, wondering what kind of horsepower it must pack. Heck of a sound to that engine. The truck was a pumper, the kind with a blocky back end, parked at an oblique angle beyond the Maxwell. The last few yards of hose were being neatly stowed into the back by two volunteer firemen who had taken off their hats in the heat.

Beyond the fire truck, two squad cars from the Minnetonka Police Department were side by side, and another squad from the Sheriff's Department beside them, with a severely plain official automobile behind them. An ambulance-sized van with HENNEPIN COUNTY MEDICAL EXAMINER painted on its door and rear end had parked between the body and the road, blocking the view of passersby. Cars on the road slowed to see what the fuss was about, naturally, but were being encouraged to move along by a cop who had put on soft white gloves to make his hands more visible. The last vehicle in the lay-by was Adam's, a midnight blue sedan. He was standing outside it, leaning against the door because he was tired of standing. He considered opening his car door and sitting down, but decided against it.

Two men in civilian dark slacks and shirts were examining the Maxwell. One was standing on the far-side running board, getting black streaks on his white shirt; the other, in a light blue shirt and dark tie, gesturing while he asked a question. He then turned to gesture at a young woman in khaki slacks and green T-shirt who was taking photographs of the back end of the car. As Adam watched, the woman climbed up on the near running board, leaning forward to take a photograph and garner her own sooty streaks, which she brushed at with a weary, used-to-it sigh.

Meanwhile, one of the men went to stoop for a closer

look at the nightmare ruin of Bill, to reach out and touch—Adam turned away again.

After a minute a voice said, "Mr. Smith?"

"Yes?" asked Adam, straightening.

"I'm Dr. Phillip Pascuzzi, with the Medical Examiner's Office. May I ask you a few questions?" The man wore a white shirt and had a notebook in one hand.

"Certainly."

"Was Mr. Birmingham a friend or relation?"

"He was a member of the Minnesota Antique Car Club, of which I am President. And he was a friend."

Writing, "And you're quite sure the body over there is, in fact, Mr. Birmingham?"

"Yes." Adam swallowed. Having to go look closely at what had been Bill Birmingham was the worst thing he'd had to do in his entire life.

"The body is badly burned, especially around the upper body. What made you sure?"

"Well, he's Bill's size, and he's wearing what Bill was wearing today, and the car is Bill's. Nobody else driving in the Run is missing. I don't see who else it could be."

"Did you talk to Mr. Birmingham today?"

"Yes, briefly."

"Where and when was this?"

"In Excelsior, this morning. He was having trouble with the car, and I said something about it, and he agreed it was running rough. As soon as he got parked along the curb, he opened the hood and began working on it. Didn't quit until it was time to start back for St. Paul. He was the last to leave because his car didn't want to start. After he left, we tore down in Excelsior and went to St. Paul to greet the cars as they came back and help them set up an exhibit over there. And when Bill didn't turn up in St. Paul, I started driving back, following the route, looking for where he broke down."

"I take it you didn't follow the route the old cars took when you went to St. Paul."

"No, we went out 7 and caught the freeway at 494."

"So Mr. Birmingham was the last to leave Excelsior on this route. Everyone else was either ahead of him or went by another way."

"Yes, that's right." The Antique Car Club had notified law enforcement agencies of the twisting route the antique cars would follow so they could come out and direct traffic or practice a little crowd control or at least be aware if there was a report of trouble involving an antique car, their choice.

"You didn't suggest that perhaps he shouldn't make the return trip?"

"No, our members usually have a pretty good idea whether or not their cars are able to continue a run. You have to realize, these cars are valuable, so most drivers are very reluctant to push a car even up to its limits. And Bill was proud of his Maxwells. I don't think he'd get stupid about making a trip when a car wasn't up to it. He tinkered with this one, and got it started and set off, so we assumed he'd be okay."

"There's a cell phone on the body. Why do you suppose he didn't call for help when he broke down?"

"We were wondering why we hadn't heard from him when he didn't come in. Probably he got to working on it and time got away from him."

"Is that also normal behavior for him?"

"Absolutely. It's a common trait among car collectors. Bill's wife complained more than once how he'd forget to come in to supper when he was out working on his cars. It's very likely the trouble he was having today got bad enough to make him pull in here, where he tried to fix it or at least get the car able to finish the run. Then he got all wrapped up in what he was doing, and somewhere in there . . . this happened."

"Have you any idea what kind of trouble he was having with the car?"

"The engine was running ragged when he drove up to the booth in Excelsior. I didn't ask him what he thought it was, I was busy. He went right to work on it, but he still had a hard time getting it started again. He finally did, though he was the last car to leave for the trip back. His wife said she was getting an upset stomach from riding in it, and she opted not to ride back with him. She rode over to St. Paul with one of my volunteers and is in St. Paul now. I don't look forward to going back there and trying to talk to her about this. We've never lost a driver during a run before."

"Not even in an accident?"

"No, never. We had a close call with a rollover, and a few other injuries—sprained wrists from hand cranking, for example, and Dick Pellow's Overland caught fire a few years ago, but he's fine. What I don't understand is, why didn't Bill get out from under when she caught on fire? Unless it blew up—I mean like parts scattered to hell and gone—which it didn't, he should've been able to at least roll away, I'd've thought."

"I'm inclined to agree with you, Mr. Smith. And there are some other oddities about this situation."

"Like what?"

"I don't want to start speculating, not without further

investigation. We are going to impound the car and there will be an autopsy on Mr. Birmingham. Perhaps you could inform Mrs. Birmingham? She can contact me at my office for further information. Do you have her phone number? I'll want to get in touch with her."

Adam read it to him off the card. Dr. Pascuzzi gave him a card with his name, the notation that he was Hennepin County's Assistant Medical Examiner, and a couple of phone and fax numbers.

"Thank you," said Adam. "Am I free to go now?"

"Yes, sir, and thank you for your cooperation."

Charlotte recovered from her faint puzzled at what had caused it, so Ceil had to tell her all over again that Bill was dead. She shrieked loudly, causing heads all over the area to turn toward her, then clapped both hands over her mouth to keep from shrieking some more. Her eyes were wide and terrified.

Betsy sat down on the blacktop beside her and pulled her head onto her shoulder. "There, there," she murmured as Charlotte began to weep noisily.

"Oh, my God," mourned Charlotte between sobs. "Oh, my God, my poor Bill! Oh, Broward will be just devastated, he and Bill worked so closely together! Oh, all my children, how can I bear to tell my children? Oh, I can't bear this!"

It was a minute or two before she felt the discomfort of her twisted position and began to pull back from it. Betsy helped her sit up straight, and took the proffered handkerchief from Mildred so Charlotte could mop her face. Her eyes were puffy and bewildered.

"Did . . . did you say it was a fire?" she asked Ceil. "He caught on *fire*?"

"Yes," nodded Ceil. "Adam said there was a fire engine there putting it out."

"A fire," repeated Charlotte, frowning. "Then why didn't he just pull over and jump out?"

"I don't know," said Betsy.

"Perhaps he meant there was an accident, and it caught fire after," said Mildred.

"Oh, yes, that must be it," said Charlotte. "Maybe a tire blew out, and he ran off the road and into a tree or telephone pole. Or did someone run into him? People do that, you know, they see the funny-looking car and steer right for it. Was there another car involved?"

Ceil said, "Adam didn't mention that."

"That stupid Maxwell! It was misbehaving all the way out there, he should never have tried to drive back. If it wasn't a tire, then I suppose something went wrong with the steering or brakes, and he ran into a ditch. And the car caught on fire, and Bill was hurt, unconscious . . . Yes, that must be it, don't you think?" She looked around at the other women for confirmation, as if figuring out what had happened would make it less dreadful.

But realization still clouded her eyes, and she began to weep again, saying over and over, "No, no, no, it's too awful, too awful."

A crowd had gathered, drawn by Charlotte's distress. Among them were members of the Antique Car Club. Ceil caught the eye of the largest of them, and semaphored a message with her eyebrows. He began to move between the onlookers and the booth, facing outward. "Drivers, go back to your cars!" he ordered in a big, loud voice. "We've still got a crowd here with questions, cameras, and sticky fingers, so move it, move it!"

He raised his hands in a backing motion. "As for the rest of you, this isn't any of your business. Please give this woman a little privacy."

The crowd broke up, and the big man leaned over the booth's counter to say to Charlotte, "I just heard. I can't tell you how sorry I am, Char. Bill was a good man, he'll be missed."

"Oh, Marcus, what am I going to *do*?" wept Charlotte.

"You relax, we'll take care of whatever needs taking care of," promised Marcus. "Do you need someone to drive you home?"

"I—I suppose so. I don't know, I can't think!"

"Never mind, you just sit here awhile, until you calm down and this show is over. I'll stay around until you decide what you want." The man strode over to a Cadillac touring car of immense size and, when he turned and saw Betsy watching him, gave a wave and a gesture of support.

"How long should I stay?" asked Charlotte of no one in particular. "Adam's been gone so long, why hasn't he come back? Why doesn't he call? Should I call him?" She seemed to be working herself into another fit of hysterics.

Betsy said, "Come on, Charlotte, let's go someplace cool and private." She helped Charlotte to her feet and said to Mildred and Ceil, "I'll sit with her in my car awhile." She repeated that to Marcus, who nodded understandingly, then went on to the parking lot around the back of the capitol.

Betsy started her engine, and the Buick's inside quickly cooled. The purring of the engine was a soothing sound, and Charlotte began to regain control of herself. "I made a fool of myself back there," she murmured, using another Kleenex from the supply Betsy kept handing her from the box she always kept in her car.

"No you didn't," said Betsy firmly. "I'm sure this has been a terrible shock to you, and I think you're taking it very well."

Charlotte made a sound halfway toward a giggle. "If this is taking it well, I wonder what taking it badly might be."

"Oh, screaming and running in circles, tearing your clothing, and throwing dirt on top of your head."

"Oh, if only it were correct in our culture to do that, what a relief it would be!" sighed Charlotte. "I really yearn to scream and kick dents into the trailer that dreadful car came in, set fire to the shed he keeps the other cars in." She amended in a small voice, "*Kept* the other cars in. Oh, dear!"

"I shouldn't go setting fire to anything until I made sure the insurance was up to date," said Betsy in a mock-practical tone.

"Oh, no fear of that," grumbled Charlotte, blowing her nose again. Her tone moderated and she became reflective. "I remember when we were first married, Bill put me in charge of the checkbook, paying bills and such. When the baby came, I was a very nervous mother and I made several long-distance calls to my mother. This was back when long-distance charges were actually scary, not like today, and my mother lived in Oregon. And when the bill came, I couldn't pay it. When Bill saw the overdue notice we got from the phone company, he hit the ceiling. He said he didn't care if we lived on day-old bread and baloney, I was not to let a bill go unpaid ever again. And I never did. Of course, as Bill's company began to thrive, that became less of a problem." She smiled just a little. "He was a good provider. We were looking forward to a long, comfortable retirement."

"He wasn't retired, then?" asked Betsy.

"Not quite. He had turned over most of the day-to-day management to Broward—he's our oldest son—but went in to the office three mornings a week, just to keep an eye on things. People like Bill never really retire, I suppose. He was thinking of organizing a new company, one that would centralize the ordering of parts for Maxwells, and perhaps do some restoration work as well. He really liked working on those cars." She sighed and sniffed—then stirred herself to take a new tack. "Your husband, what does he think of you owning your own business?"

"I'm divorced," said Betsy. "I inherited the shop after the divorce. My sister founded it. And her husband was proud of her, though at first he didn't take her seriously. You know how men are, or how they used to be, anyway. He thought of it like a hobby, a way of keeping the little woman busy."

"Yes, I know," said Charlotte, with some feeling. "Did you help your husband in his business?"

"I was in sales for several years at the start, until I got pregnant with Broward. I was pretty good at sales, and I liked it. But he wanted me to stay at home, and before I knew it, there I was with four children, and no time for anything outside the home. Not that I minded too terribly. Our children were a great pleasure always, reasonably good kids, very bright. Lisa won several scholarships and is a pediatrician in St. Louis. Tommy owns a car dealership in St. Paul, and David is working on his masters in education at the U. But after the youngest left home, I wanted to do something more, get a job, but Bill was too used to me being home. Do you have children?"

"No, it turned out I couldn't get pregnant."

"I'm sorry."

"It turned out I couldn't pick a good man to father them either, so it's just as well. Are you close to your children?"

"Oh, yes, of course. It's going to be hard on them, losing their father all of a sudden like this. Broward and Bill were especially close, working together like they did."

"What sort of company is it?"

"It's called Birmingham Metal Fabrication. We make doors, metal doors, for houses and apartments, garages, and businesses. We sell to builders mostly. Broward's been wanting to expand into window frames and maybe even siding. He's very ambitious."

"Perhaps you could get back into sales, working for your son."

"Perhaps." Charlotte let her head fall back on the headrest. "All that crying has given me a terrible headache."

Someone knocked on the window and Charlotte jumped. "What, what?" she cried. "Oh, it's Adam!" She began to fumble with the door. "How do I roll the window down?" she demanded.

Betsy pushed a button on her side, and the window slid down about eight inches. Adam's anxious face peered in at them.

"Hello, Betsy," he said. "Charlotte, may I talk to you a minute?"

"Is something else wrong?"

"Well, I'm not sure."

"What do you mean, you're not sure? What's wrong, what's happened?"

Adam said uncomfortably, "Well, the medical examiner was there, he and the police looked at the scene, and they seem to think there's something funny about what happened. Here—" Adam handed her a business card. "This is the medical examiner's name and phone number. You can call him when you feel up to it, though he said he would be in touch anyway. He's going to do an autopsy, and they've impounded the Maxwell."

"Something funny?" echoed Charlotte. "What could that mean?"

"I have no idea, they wouldn't tell me what they're thinking."

"What could be funny about Bill's dying in his car?" Charlotte turned to look at Betsy. "What do you think?"

"I don't know," said Betsy, afraid to say the word that was big in all their minds: Murder.

7

Monday morning, Betsy was preparing an order of stitched items to be sent to Heidi, her finisher. A Christmas stocking done on needlepoint canvas, stiff with metallic threads and beads, needed to be washed, stretched and shaped, cut out, lined, and sewn to a heavy fabric so it would be a proper stocking. A highly detailed counted cross stitch pattern of a Queen Anne house needed washing, stretching, and attachment to a stretcher before being matted and framed. There were five other items needing finishing, two to be made into pillows. Some needleworkers finished their own projects, but many turned to a professional. It was expensive, but gave a proper finish to a needlework project that its proud owner hoped would become an heirloom.

Last on the list of items to be finished was an original Irene Potter. Name of owner: Betsy Devonshire. Betsy had gone to the art fair on Sunday—and been disappointed to find the amazing Columbus Circle Blizzard piece Irene had brought half-shyly to Crewel World had been sold. However, there were three other pieces on display, and Betsy, wincing only slightly, had written a check for a piece called Walled Garden, a riot of color and stitches about sixteen by sixteen inches, done in brightly colored wool, silk, ribbon, cotton, and metallics on stiff congress cloth. There was a pond in the center, worked in irregular half-stitches of blue silk and silver metallic floss. A single orange stitch suggested a goldfish in its depths. A rustic wooden bridge crossed the pond, leading to a winding path among daisies, azaleas, daffodils, lilies, and many other varieties of flowers, some invented, done with no regard to season or proportion or perspective. In the upper background, the waving limbs of mighty trees threatened to crush or climb the wall, which was braced here and there by slender young poplars. Outside the wall a hurricane raged. Within was a hot, strangely lit, tense silence.

The work made Betsy feel she was looking into Irene's mind, or perhaps Irene's notion of the world. Whichever, it was a place both beautiful and frightening.

"Oh, my *God*, what is *that*?" demanded Godwin, reaching for the piece.

Betsy started to explain, then changed her mind. "What do you think?" she asked.

"It's wonderful, it's . . . what a garden must seem like to the plants. Who stitched this—no, who *designed* it?"

"It's another Irene Potter," said Betsy. "I bought it at the art fair."

Godwin tenderly fingered the stitching of the garden

wall, done in shades of red, garnet, and brown in a herringbone stitch that looked like bricks laid in Tudor fashion. The formal wall formed an orderly base for the tree branches tossing in bullion and wildly irregular continental stitches. In front of the wall were stiffly formal blooming shrubs worked in—what? He looked closer. Fancy cross? No, a variety of half-buttonhole.

"I am humbled," he said sincerely. "This is totally amazing." He handed it back. "You're having it framed, I assume."

"Yes, but in something severe, I think. Narrow cream mat, thin black frame? Because the work is so hot and wild."

"Sounds good." Godwin looked around. "Where are you going to hang it?"

"Upstairs. This isn't a model. Irene says she can't turn these pieces into patterns."

"Bosh," retorted Godwin. "If she can stitch it, she or someone can make a pattern of it. They'd be difficult patterns, but not impossible ones. She just doesn't want to share. I don't blame her, I guess. Do you realize this confirms she's turning into an artist with a capital A?"

"Oh, yes. And so does she. You should have seen her at the fair, preening and talking with vast condescension to anyone who stopped to look at her work. But she's earned the right, her work is wonderful. She brought nine pieces to the fair and sold all of them. Mr. Feldman is now taking her very seriously indeed; he was asking three or four thousand apiece."

"You paid how much?"

"Thirty-five hundred for this. I know that's a lot—"

"She should have given you a discount."

"No, she shouldn't. We've laughed too often at her

expense. Besides, this is really wonderful. I think it's worth the price. Plus, it's only going to increase in value. Irene said the Walker Art Museum bought one, and a reporter from the *Strib* wants to interview her. If this keeps up, a local employer is going to lose the head of its shipping department very soon."

"Maybe I should bring them my résumé."

"Why would you do that?"

"Because I am going to need a job with benefits. Betsy, I talked with John yesterday. He started shouting at me, right there in the restaurant—" Godwin sobbed once, gulped it back, and continued, "And I got hysterical and ran out. And . . . and he didn't come after me. He just let me *go*!"

"Oh, Goddy," sighed Betsy, putting an arm around his shoulder.

He suddenly twisted around to embrace her, soaking her shoulder with hot tears. "Betsy, what am I to *do*? I don't know how I'm going to live without our darling house, and having wonderful clothes and traveling, and him taking care of me . . ." His voice trailed away, and then he pushed himself away to stare at Betsy aghast, his eyes still shining with tears. "Oh, my *God*! It's happened. Donny told me it would happen, and it *has*!"

"What's happened?" asked Betsy.

"The *Golden Handcuffs*! I don't miss *John*, I miss all the *things*! John got me used to nice things, and now I'm upset because I'm losing the things, not because I'm losing *John*!"

If Godwin hadn't been so sincere, Betsy would have

laughed at him. As it was, she couldn't withhold a smile. "Oh, Goddy," she sighed.

"What?" he said, and when she didn't answer at once, he demanded, "What? Tell me!"

"Well . . . I'm afraid I always thought what you and John had was an arrangement, not a relationship. Now I've only met John once, but he didn't impress me as a very nice person. And I've never met anyone who seemed to actually like John. So I guess—" She broke off, afraid she was getting into dangerous waters. "Let's not go there."

"No, no," said Godwin, suddenly very serious, more serious than she'd ever seen him. "Tell me."

"I don't know how to say it, or even whether I should say anything at all."

Godwin's eyes gleamed, though his expression remained serious. "I think it's important that you try to tell me anyway."

"Well, I've always known gay people, and some were friends. But I've never met a gay person before who was as much like the old stereotype of the gay man as you are. I'd gotten to thinking no real gay person was like that, until you came along. So . . . well, I sometimes wonder if it's really you, either. I mean, I wonder if maybe I've never really met the real Godwin. I've wondered if this is a put-on, that you only pretend to be this person who is solely interested in clothes and parties and startling straight people. Now I like that fun and funny persona, and it's extremely valuable here in the shop. But is this surface Godwin . . . perhaps too frivolous to be real? I sometimes wonder what you're like when it's late at night and you're tired. Or what you might be like when the party comes to an end. I've never tried to dig into your personality, because I like the surface Godwin very much, and because that Goddy has been so useful to me. I wonder if that was wrong of me, because I think of you as a friend."

"And because maybe you were afraid that's the only me there is?" asked Godwin with a little smile.

"Not afraid, just wondering. You know me, I can't help wondering if things are as they seem. But I don't want you to feel you have to act serious just to make me think you're deep."

Godwin shrugged. "I suppose there is another me down inside somewhere, but he's not nearly as much fun as this upper me. Being the fun Goddy *is* fun. And it's taken me a long way. Being serious is . . . *serious.* And not much fun. See how my vocabulary suffers when I try to be serious?" He grinned. "So that's enough depth plumbing for today. Why didn't you buy the Columbus Circle Blizzard piece?"

"I couldn't, it was the first thing sold on Saturday." Betsy took Walled Garden back and held it in both hands. "But I like this one too."

"Speaking of Saturday—" began Godwin, but was interrupted by the electronic *Bing!* that announced the door to the shop opening.

They looked up and saw a tall, very slender man standing just inside the door. He wore a lightweight gray suit, white shirt, and dark blue tie. He looked to be close to sixty, with thin silver hair, a bit of a stoop, and a diffident, thoughtful expression somewhat at odds with his stuck-out ears and humorous narrow jaw.

He glanced at Godwin, and took in his whole life story in a single intelligent look. His smile was friendly, with a hint of amusement in it.

Godwin, not sure whether to be affronted, stood fast.

Then the man looked at Betsy and the smile broadened into a sideways grin. "I bet you own this place," he said in a reedy voice too young for his years, gesturing around with a large, thin hand.

"That's right," said Betsy, wondering why alarms were sounding in her head. He certainly looked harmless enough. "Is there something I can help you with?"

"I certainly hope so." He came to the big desk, fumbling in an inside pocket for a slim wallet. Only it wasn't a wallet, it was an identification holder. Opened, it told Betsy he was Detective Morrie Steffans, Minnetonka Police. "I've been talking with Mrs. Charlotte Birmingham, and she says you can confirm that she was with you most of Saturday."

Alarms now sounding loud indeed, Betsy said, "Why do you need that confirmed?"

"Weren't you with her when she was told there were unanswered questions about the death of her husband and the burning of his car?" He put the wallet away and brought out a thick, palm-size notebook and a ballpoint pen.

"Yes—I take it some of the questions have been answered?"

He grinned. He had very light blue eyes and good teeth. "I take it she hasn't contacted you since she talked with me?"

"Why should she contact me?" asked Betsy. "Will you tell me what this is about?"

"Certainly, as soon as I get some basic information from you." He took Betsy's name, address, and phone number, then said, "It seems that the late Mr. Birmingham was shot in the chest before being put under that old car of his."

"Oh, my," murmured Betsy. "How terrible."

"Shot?" echoed Godwin. "You mean he was *murdered*?" He said accusingly to Betsy, "You didn't say there was anything funny about his death!"

"I didn't know there was, not for certain," replied Betsy. "None of us did." To Detective Steffans, she said, "So I take it the car didn't catch fire by itself, either."

"That's right, it was torched. A clumsy attempt was made to make it look like an accident, but this was clearly homicide."

"Or suicide," suggested Godwin.

Detective Steffans frowned at Godwin. "Why would someone crawl under a car, set it on fire, and then shoot himself?"

"Oh," said Godwin.

Detective Steffans said to Betsy, "You talked with Mr. Birmingham?"

"Yes, we exchanged a few words," replied Betsy. "I was a volunteer for the Antique Car Club, and they assigned me the task of logging the arrival of the antique cars in Excelsior. I wrote down their number and time of arrival, and instructed the drivers to report to the booth. Mr. Birmingham didn't say much, but I could see he was upset because his car was running badly, so I talked mostly with his wife, Charlotte. I did tell him reporters were here and might want to interview him, and he said he didn't want to answer questions."

"Had you met Mr. Birmingham before?"

"No."

"But you're sure it was him."

"Well, Charlotte seemed sure, and she was his wife."

Steffans chuckled and made a note. "You've never met Charlotte before, have you?"

"No. Are you going to tell me you don't think the woman was Mrs. Birmingham?"

"No, of course not. I'm at that stage of my investigation where I check everything. However, I am satisfied that it was Mr. and Mrs. Birmingham in the car. And I'm asking if it was during the halt in Excelsior that you and Mrs. Birmingham struck up an acquaintance."

Betsy nodded. "Yes, she came into my shop and spent a nice amount of money, and helped me log the drivers out of town when they left. Adam Smith asked her to assist me. She didn't want to ride in the Maxwell anymore, because the engine running so rough made it jiggle, which upset her stomach."

Steffans nodded. "Leaf springs."

"I beg your pardon?"

"Leaf springs, from before shock absorbers. Smooth out the bumps, but can't dampen the jiggle."

Betsy nodded. "All right. Anyway, Charlotte rode with me to St. Paul, and helped me again when we logged in the drivers on the return leg. Bill Birmingham's Maxwell didn't come in, and we didn't hear from him, so after a while Adam left to drive the route looking for him. Charlotte sat with me in the booth in St. Paul until Adam called Ceil—that's Lucille Ziegfield, a member of the club—and Ceil told Charlotte that Bill was dead. Charlotte was very upset, of course. I took her to my car—"

"Why?" interrupted Steffans.

"Because she was crying and people were staring.

And we both were hot. She was wearing an old-fashioned dress and a big antique hat, so she was more uncomfortable than I was. So I took her to my car, started it, and turned on the air-conditioning, and we sat and talked until Adam Smith arrived to tell us that Bill's body was taken for an autopsy because the police weren't satisfied it was an accident. She left about half an hour later. Her son Broward came and picked her up."

"And you stayed with her that whole time?"

"Yes, she was in no state to be left alone. Broward came with his wife, who seems like a very nice woman. She kind of gathered poor Charlotte in and Broward drove them away."

"What was your impression of Charlotte Birmingham?"

"I liked her. She seemed to be a nice person. Interesting company. Good needleworker. She's really into this period thing; she not only wore the correct clothes for her ride, even the needlework pattern she was working was period."

"Did she seem to be upset or distressed in any way before you learned of Mr. Birmingham's death?"

"No. Well, she got worried when his car didn't come in. And annoyed that he didn't call on his cell phone to say where he was and what the problem was."

"You saw the two of them together, however briefly. What was her attitude toward her husband?"

"Affectionate. Indulgent."

" 'Indulgent.' That's an interesting choice of word." Steffans's blue eyes searched her face, but not unkindly.

"Is it? Well, maybe it is. I was just thinking of how she said something to him that showed she understood he was feeling grumpy and was willing to do her bit to make him feel better."

"What was that?"

"When they first arrived in Excelsior, they stopped beside me. He was holding the steering wheel like grim death, jaw sort of set, because the car was misbehaving. And she said she was going to get out of the car and take off a layer of clothing—she was wearing an old-fashioned long white dress with a long coat over it—"

"A duster, I think they're called."

"Yes, that's right, a duster. Well, she looked very hot in it, so it wasn't surprising that she wanted to shed a few layers. He didn't say a word, but then she didn't get out, she said she'd ride with him up to the booth where Adam would tell them where to park. You know how people who have been married awhile can tell what the other one wants without him having to say a word? It was like that. He didn't want to talk to anyone, so she agreed she'd stay with him and talk to Adam and anyone else. Even though he didn't ask her to. She wasn't grumpy herself about it, but kind of cheerful. So I guess that's where 'indulgent' comes from."

Steffans smiled at her. "Very perceptive. You paint a very clear picture of what happened. Thank you." He consulted his notebook and asked, "You're sure that Charlotte was with you the entire time between her and her husband's arrival in Excelsior and the time you got word that he was dead?"

Betsy thought. "Well, there was that time between her and Bill's arrival and the time I clocked in the last car, turned in my clipboard, and went into my shop, where we introduced ourselves again. I didn't recognize her out of that hat and duster. But we saw Bill again after that. She went to tell him she wasn't riding back with him, and I went with her. He was working on the car, and was still unhappy. She took her duster, hat, and carpet bag out of the back seat of the car and we went to the booth. From then on she was with me."

"You saw Bill Birmingham leave Excelsior?"

"Yes, Charlotte was helping me log departure times. He was the last one to leave, because he had a lot of trouble getting the car started. He'd go to the driver's side and make some kind of adjustment then come back to the front end and yank the crank around, then make another adjustment, and crank again."

"Retarding the spark, I think it's called."

"Yes, that's right, advancing and retarding the spark. Not that it helped much. I'm surprised he didn't fall down from heat exhaustion, bundled up as he was."

"He wore a duster, too?"

"Oh, yes, and a hat—what's it called, pinch-brim? The soft kind where the crown is high in back and comes down over the bill in front. And goggles, great big old-fashioned goggles. About all you could see of his head was his mouth and chin and a bit of dark hair around the edges. He looked very authentic, and very warm. He'd open the hood and do something under there, then start in again, advancing the spark and cranking. Someone passing him on his way out of town yelled, 'You need to get a bigger hammer, Bill!' and laughed. Charlotte said that's the usual joke, get a bigger hammer."

"I thought it was 'Get a horse!'"

"No, that was what people who didn't drive back in the old days would say. Or so Charlotte told me. She knew a lot about the old cars and that time period. Her dress and hat weren't reproductions, but the real thing. She said she collected antique clothes."

"But she didn't try to help Mr. Birmingham fix the car."

"No, she said she deliberately didn't learn much about the engines and—and transmission bands, that's one term she used. She didn't want to ruin her hands working on the cars."

"All right, thank you. You've been very helpful."

After Steffans had left, Godwin said, "You didn't tell me you were mixed up in another murder."

"I didn't know until just now that I was. And anyway, you might be right about the suicide."

Godwin's eyebrows lifted in surprise. "You think so?"

Betsy nodded. "I was thinking about the insurance. You know, the suicide clause, the company won't pay off if you kill yourself?"

"Oh, of course," said Godwin. "So you're thinking he might have committed suicide and tried to make it look like an accident. Or how about he just shoots himself, and someone found his body and put it under the car and set the fire so it would look like an accident, so his widow could get the insurance."

Betsy said, "The problem with that is, who would do such a thing? And he was seen in St. Paul that morning, he was seen in Excelsior, and he was the last driver to leave on the return run. So it must have happened while he was on that return run. Except everyone involved in the run was either driving in it ahead of him or took the freeway to St. Paul after he left. So it would have to be a stranger who came along and found him—and why would a stranger do that?"

"Yeah, that would be the question, all right."

A customer came in at that point, and Godwin went to help her, leaving Betsy to think some more. She and Charlotte had waited quite a while in St. Paul for Adam and the others to arrive. Could one of them have gone after Bill? Or could someone ahead of Bill in the run have pulled into that lay-by and waited for Bill to come along?

It looked as if the only person with a solid alibi was Charlotte. Interesting.

8

At two, the Monday Bunch gathered. There were five members present, which surprised Martha. "I guess they haven't been watching the news," she said. Normally all twelve members turned out when there was a crime to discuss.

"Why, what did we miss?" asked Phil Galvin, retired railroad engineer. He was short and gray, with a round face and eyes, small, work-thickened hands, and a loud, rough voice. He was working on a counted cross stitch pattern of Native Americans in war paint riding bareback alongside an old steam locomotive.

Martha explained, "During that antique car race on Saturday, a car caught on fire in Minnetonka, killed the driver. His name was William Birmingham."

Phil nodded. "Birmingham. Yeah, I heard about that. Too bad they ain't makin' any more of those old cars."

Betsy frowned at Phil. Though the old man prided himself on his tough-guy attitude, she felt this was going too far.

Martha said, "Well, it turns out the driver was shot, not burned to death. It's a murder case. The police came and talked to Betsy, because she was the alibi for the man's wife. The wife was with Betsy all the time between when the man left here and when he was found dead."

Phil exclaimed, "No! I didn't hear about that!" He grimaced and mumbled, "Well, that makes a difference, I guess."

Martha said, surprised, "Betsy, you were on the news?"

Betsy smiled. "No, that part was spread locally." She looked at Godwin, who had the grace to blush.

Alice said, "So what do you think, Betsy? Who would shoot Bill Birmingham?"

Betsy answered with a question. "Did you know him?"

"Not personally, but I know about him. He grew up over in Wildwood, so there are probably locals who do." Wildwood was one of those Hennepin County "cities" on Lake Minnetonka that was really barely a village. It was only seven miles from Excelsior.

"I'm from Wildwood," said Phil. "I knew the whole family. In fact, I went to school with his older brother."

"What were they like?" asked Betsy.

Phil began emphatically, "Their father was the biggest—uh-ah!" He skidded to a halt, recalling who his audience was. "That is, he was one of those men thinks he was born to be boss. Couldn't stand to be disagreed with. Every kid in town, including his own, was scared of him. But both his sons grew up to be a lot like him. The older one got a double dose of it. He thought he was smarter than his teachers or anyone else who tried to teach him anything. Dropped out of high school, got fired from six jobs in seven months. He tried to kill a man he thought was after his wife, got sent to Stillwater, where he wound up knifed to death by a fellow inmate. He was twenty-six when it happened, and left a widow with a baby girl.

"Now Bill, he was different. He was a hard worker like his dad, but he was smart, and he didn't have a bad temper like his brother. He graduated from Cal Tech, and soon after invented an improved metal-stamping machine. He started a business stamping out all kinds of small metal parts, and eventually settled down to make metal doors. But he was also like his dad in that once he figured out how to do something, then that was the best way to do it, and the only way it could be done. His oldest son majored in engineering with a minor in business, but when the boy came back to go into business with his dad, the old man wouldn't listen to any of his ideas. So Broward went off to another company, bigger than his father's, and became a vice president in charge of production."

Betsy said, "But Charlotte told me Broward was working for his father, and was at the point of taking over Bill's company, since Bill was about to retire."

Phil nodded. "Yes, about two years ago, Bill's doctor warned him for the fourth or fifth time to retire or die in harness, and this time Bill believed him. He asked Bro to please come and take over. And Bro did. Quit his job and came home. Only Bill couldn't let go; he'd go to the office and make some decisions without consulting Bro—or even undo some of what Bro was doing. Drove Bro nuts, not least because Bro is a chip off the old block, and doesn't take kindly to having his decisions trifled with." Phil picked up his Wild West cross stitch piece. "It'll be interesting now to see if Bro really does have some better ideas."

Alice asked in her blunt way, "So what do you think, Betsy—Broward Birmingham murdered his father?"

Betsy said, "I don't know. Phil, does Broward share his father's interest in antique cars?"

Phil shook his head. "All he'll be interested in is how much they'll bring at auction. He knows something about them, the whole family does, but he's not interested in owning one. Charlotte knows a lot because she believes in sharing her husband's interests, plus she likes dressing up in those old-fashioned clothes, but she's strictly a passenger. Her offspring would likely be more interested if Bill had let them drive once in a while, or shared the restoration work instead of only letting them hand him the tools, but as it is, the cars will probably be sold."

"What are they worth, I wonder?" said Alice.

"I understand the Maxwells were a very popular car, and a lot of them are still around," said Betsy. "So not as much as something rarer. Still, Charlotte said there are six of them, so that's got to amount to money. I suppose they're from different years. I wonder when they went out of business."

"They didn't," said Phil. "Walter P. Chrysler bought the company in 1923 and didn't change the name until 1926."

"Oh," said Martha, amused, "then the mayor's cute PT Cruiser is really a . . . Maxwell?" They all laughed.

Except Kate. "What's so funny?" asked Kate, the youngest member.

"Rochester used to drive Jack Benny around in an old Maxwell," chortled Godwin. "Mel Blanc had all kinds of fun making the noises of that car on a radio show. Mr. Mayor will be pleased to hear that, I _don't_ think!"

"Who's Jack Benny?"

After an initial astonished pause, everyone took turns talking about Jack Benny, his awful violin playing, his comic miserliness, his futile aggravation, but it was Godwin who got to imitate Mr. Benny's most famous bit, when the robber stuck out a gun and gave him the traditional choice: "Your money or your life!" And Godwin put one hand on his cheek and fell silent while the giggles grew and grew, finally blurting, "I'm thinking, I'm thinking!"

Kate, laughing, said, "That'd be even funnier if Joe Mickels were driving one!" Joe's authentic miserliness was well known.

"Well, he does own an antique car," said Betsy.

"Is it a Maxwell?" asked Godwin, prepared to laugh.

"No, it's a . . ." Betsy thought. "A McIntyre."

Godwin said in a hurt voice, "Betsy, you've taken to keeping things from me."

"I'd forgotten all about it," said Betsy, and she related the tale of Adam Smith and Joe Mickels maneuvering around one another over the possible sale of Joe's McIntyre. "Adam collects rare cars, and this is very rare."

"Must be," said Phil. "I never heard of that brand. It'll be interesting to see who skins who in that deal."

Forty minutes later, the Bunch started picking up and

putting away. The door went *Bing!* and everyone turned to see Charlotte Birmingham in the doorway, her sewing bag in her hand and a shy look on her face. She was dressed in darkness, black shoes, dark stockings, a severely plain black dress. There were even dark shadows under her eyes.

Betsy stood. "Hello, Mrs. Birmingham," she said. "Is there something I can do for you?"

"It looks as if your meeting is breaking up," replied Charlotte, coming toward the table. "I was hoping to join you." She looked the very opposite of the friendly woman in white Betsy had met on Saturday, more ravaged than the shocked and bewildered woman who had sat in her car later that same day.

"I'm afraid you're a little late," said Betsy, shaking herself out of her stare. "We meet at two, and it's nearly three-thirty."

"Oh, I thought you met at three," said Charlotte. "How stupid of me not to have phoned to check that!"

"Well, since you drove all that distance, why don't you stay at least for a little while," said Betsy. "Perhaps Godwin can sit with you for a while."

"I don't have to leave right now," said Phil, who was retired.

"Me, either," said Alice, sitting back down.

The other women left—reluctantly, because they were going to miss something to gossip about. Charlotte got out a counted cross stitch pattern of her son's name done in an alphabet by Lois Winston. It had little engineer's tools worked into the letters: a compass, a T square, a level. Betsy remembered seeing the pattern in *The Cross Stitcher* magazine.

"It's for Broward's office door," said Charlotte.

While Charlotte talked quietly with Godwin, Phil, and Alice, Betsy began the task of pulling the wool needed for a needlepoint canvas a woman had called to say she wanted after all. The canvas was a Constance Coleman rendition of a Scottish terrier looking out a big window at a winter scene that included a stag. Betsy enjoyed the task of finding just the right colors and textures to suit the painting—Very Velvet for the deer, Wisper for the terrier, shades of maroon wool for the chintz curtains. She considered the problem of the windowsill. Something vaguely shiny, maybe, to echo the lacquer finish of the paint?

Bing! went the front door, and Betsy looked around to see Phil and Alice heading up the street. She looked over and saw Charlotte bent over her needlework and Godwin signalling Betsy by raising and lowering his eyebrows.

"Goddy," said Betsy obediently, "could you come look at this? I can't decide what would do for the woodwork, and we need something creative for the snow. You know how Mrs. Hampton is." And in fact, she would complain if the fibers weren't clever enough.

"Certainly," said Godwin just as if he hadn't been desperate for her to summon him. He came over and, under cover of looking at the canvas, murmured, "She wants to talk to you about something. She keeps looking around for you and sighing."

"All right. But do finish getting this ready. Mrs. Hampton will be by to pick it up soon."

"All right."

Betsy went to sit down across from Charlotte. "I hope you aren't finding all the terrible details of your husband's death too much for you," she said.

"No, I'm lucky to have my children all rallying around to help," Charlotte said. "Lisa has been a great comfort to me, and Broward has taken over most of the work. All I do is sign where he tells me to sign, and try to decide where we are going to ask contributions to be sent in lieu of flowers." She smiled sadly. "But still I feel all off balance, like half of me is gone."

"That's what happens when a good marriage ends, I'm told," said Betsy. "It will pass, and you'll have some wonderful memories."

"So my children tell me. The sad part is, we were building some new wonderful memories, going to a much better place in our marriage, but we never got a chance to finish the journey." She bowed her head. "I am *so angry* about that! This should be a time of mourning, and instead I am angry. And I am angry about being made angry." Her upside-down smile reappeared. "And isn't that ridiculous? Being angry because I've been left angry."

"I'm so sorry," said Betsy, not knowing what else to say.

"But I didn't come here to talk about my sorrows. In fact, I was looking for a little time away from all that, and here I sit talking and talking about it. But I do want to thank you for taking me under your wing on Saturday. As it turned out, it was more than kind. The police were looking rather sideways at me until they found out you were with me all through the . . . important hours."

"I'm glad I could be of service," said Betsy. "It was shocking to hear that your husband was killed. I remember how angry I was when my sister was murdered, too, so your anger is very understandable to me."

Charlotte put down her needlework to confide, "The

worst part is learning that someone hated Bill so much he felt the only way to handle it was to kill him. I know Bill could be difficult, but lots of people are difficult. *I'm* difficult at times. That's no reason to kill! I can't figure out what Bill might have done to make someone hate him enough to shoot him. It makes me feel as if my whole world is constructed of very thin boards over a very deep hole."

"There is no need for you to feel like that. In fact, it's just as well you don't know why. If you knew why, perhaps the murderer would come after you."

Charlotte stared at Betsy. "Are you trying to frighten me?"

"No, of course not!" said Betsy hastily. "On the contrary! The fact that you can't think of anyone angry enough at Bill to shoot him means it doesn't involve you at all. It's probably about his work, or something from his past."

"Not his work, not his work," protested Charlotte.

"Why not?"

"Because that might involve my son Broward. And he can't have anything to do with this, he just can't."

"All right," said Betsy, deciding Charlotte was not in any condition to seriously consider who might have done this terrible deed, if she was willing to let desire overwhelm fact. "I'm sorry you missed the Monday Bunch. Perhaps you can come again next Monday? I'd love to have you join us." Betsy stood. She had a lot of work to do.

"Wait a minute," said Charlotte, gesturing at her to sit down again. "Betsy, is it true that you have a talent for solving crimes?"

Obediently, Betsy sat. "Yes. But you don't want me to look into this."

"I don't?"

"No, because you are already afraid of what might be found out."

"No, I'm not." But Charlotte's face was afraid—and suddenly she seemed to realize that, and smiled. "Well, perhaps I am, a little. I suppose it can't be helped that the police will find out things that are better hidden. That's why I'm here, really. When the police find things out, it gets into the newspapers. But you can find things out and maybe only tell the police things that will lead to the murderer."

"My looking into this case won't stop the police looking as well. And anyway, what if it turns out the murderer is someone you don't want found out?"

Charlotte said very firmly, "I am perfectly sure that won't happen."

Godwin, who had been lurking with intent to eavesdrop, could no longer resist. "There are some people in prison right now who were perfectly sure an amateur sleuth couldn't possibly figure out what they'd done."

Charlotte looked around indignantly, but Godwin smiled and said gently, "I think that if you have a secret you don't want revealed, whether about yourself or someone else, you should either tell her right now what it is, or change your mind about asking her to look into things. She will find it out."

"Yes, but it won't become part of an official file, or turn up in the newspaper." She looked at Betsy. "Please, please help me. Help preserve the reputation of my family."

"Is there something bad about your family the police can find out about?"

"No!" said Charlotte, too sharply. Then, "Well, yes. Do I have to tell you what it is?"

"Might it have given someone a motive to murder your husband?"

"No," said Charlotte.

"Then I don't need to know."

After she had left, Godwin said, "So you're going to look into this."

"Looks like it."

"I wonder what the big secret is."

"I suspect it has something to do with her son. And remember what Phil said, about Bro and his father struggling for control of the steel door company. Do you know anything about the company?"

"It's Birmingham Metal Fabrication of Roseville, I know that. Our back door was made by them. Our decorator recommended them, but he always wants us to buy local."

"So you don't know if it's in good financial condition."

"No. But I'd think a quarrel in the uppermost management couldn't be a good thing."

"Yes, that's true. But was the quarrel serious enough to lead to murder? That's the real question."

9

First thing Tuesday morning a man in a handsome three-piece business suit came into Crewel World. Despite the vest, and though his shirt had long sleeves with French cuffs held together with heavy gold links, and his bright blue silk tie was tight against his collar, he did not look the least wilted in the early-morning warmth and humidity. The big American sedan he'd climbed out of in front of the shop was a variety that came with heavy air-conditioning.

He was tall, with dark brown hair and blue eyes, square-jawed and handsome, moving with athletic grace. The fit of the suit bespoke wealth. Betsy could almost hear Godwin's engine start to race.

But the man ignored Godwin's flutter of inquiring eyelashes and came to the desk to ask Betsy, "Are you Ms. Devonshire?"

"Yes, that's right."

"I'm Broward Birmingham." He didn't hold out his hand, and his tone was that of an executive seriously thinking that order could be restored only by firing someone. Betsy suddenly realized that his jaw was so prominent because the underlying muscles were clenched.

"How do you do?" said Betsy.

"My mother came here yesterday and talked with you." It was not a question.

"Yes, she did."

"She asked you to do some unofficial investigating of the murder of my father."

"That's correct."

"I am here to ask you not to do that."

"Why not?"

"Because this isn't any of your business. I see no reason to ask an amateur to second-guess the police."

"Actually, I wouldn't be second-guessing them. I don't have any idea what they might be doing. I will just talk to people, listen to their stories, and draw my own conclusions."

"And who knows what conclusions an amateur might draw? This isn't something you've been trained to do."

"That's true. But I seem to have a talent for it. Also, I am unhampered by the rules—of evidence and so forth—that the police must follow."

"That is exactly why I am asking you to stay out of this. I don't want you screwing up an official investigation."

"I wouldn't dream of doing that!"

"I'm sure you wouldn't, not on purpose. On the other hand, if you come across evidence and handle it or move it or take it away, that can compromise the rules that must be followed for the evidence to be used in a court of law."

"Oh, I see what you're getting at. But, you see, I wouldn't do something like that. I have a friend who is a police officer, and she advises me about particulars like that. I don't usually pick up things, mostly I just talk with people. It can't hurt to talk."

"I'm not just concerned about you moving evidence. I don't want you to investigate, period. Let me tell you as plainly as I know how: Stay out of this."

Betsy nearly continued arguing with him. Then she saw that the muscles in his jaw were even more prominent, and she recalled what Phil had said yesterday about the Birmingham men: They don't like people to disagree with them.

Broward had no legal authority over Betsy, but something her mother used to say rolled across the front of her mind on those letters made of dots: *Those who fight and run away, live to fight another day.*

"I understand," she said as meekly as she could, and dropped her eyes.

"Thank you," he said tightly, turned on his heel, and walked out.

Godwin withheld his snigger until Broward slammed himself into his big car and drove away. "Good for you," he said. Because Betsy had not said she was going to obey Broward's order, only that she understood it.

"I wonder how long I'll be able to poke around before he finds out?"

Godwin's amused smile faded as he thought that

over. "I think you ought to be even more concerned about what he'll do when he *does* find out."

Adam Smith sat at the head of the old wooden table, his six steering committee members arranged down either side. Five were, like him, white males in their sixties. The sixth was Ceil Ziegfield, married to a white male in his sixties. Every one of them owned at least one antique car; every one had made the New London to New Brighton run at least three times.

Adam had tried it fourteen times in six different cars, and had finished it only nine. He liked the rarer makes, which tended to be more delicate, eccentric, and cranky than the ones which had proved their worth by becoming numerous. But he always had chosen the road less traveled.

"Have we got all the pretour routes printed?" Drivers would gather in New London early, and would drive to nearby towns: Paynesville on Wednesday, Spicer on Thursday, and Litchfield on Friday, following complicated routes on back roads, trying to keep off busy highways as much as possible.

"All set," said Ceil. She was secretary of the committee, naturally; it never occurred to the men to think a woman wouldn't be pleased to take minutes and do the endless paperwork connected with this project. Ceil wasn't pleased. On the other hand, the men who had done the job in previous years—this was the first year a woman had been honored by being chosen to sit on the steering committee—had managed all right, and so she supposed she could, too.

"Who's going out ahead to put up arrows?" asked Ed.

"Me, I guess," said Adam. Small squares of paper with bold black arrows printed on them were to be stapled on fence posts at intersections to aid drivers. This had been the late Bill Birmingham's job, as he had been in charge of laying out this year's routes.

But after a discussion about possible problems Adam might have to be on site to resolve, it was decided that Jerry, who had laid out the routes last year, should put up the arrows. Ceil handed over the shoebox full of them and a staple gun.

"What else?" asked Adam. "What have we forgotten?" There was always something forgotten, something that was thought to have been taken care of that wasn't, some glitch in the planning. This would be the Sixteenth Annual New London to New Brighton Antique Car Run, but he was sure that even now, after sixteen years, there was a screwup somewhere.

But everyone turned confident smiles on him, and Ceil even said aloud, "Nothing. Everything's fine."

"We have enough banners," Adam prompted, meaning the heavy plastic squares with a soft drink logo and a number on them—a past president of the club owned a soft drink bottling company, and supplied the banners for free, complete with logo.

"We have fifty-three drivers signed up as of yesterday evening, and expect perhaps twelve more by Saturday," said Ed, consulting his notes. People were allowed to sign up as late as the day of the run. "We've never had more than seventy, and we have banners numbered up to eighty-five."

"Have we got enough volunteers at Buffalo High for lunch?" Buffalo wasn't a big city, but the high school was one of those massive consolidated ones, with a huge parking lot. Drivers came in for a hot lunch of hamburgers and hot dogs, with cole slaw and watermelon on the side. The Antique Car Club had to rent the cafeteria from the school district, and then find volunteers to buy supplies and prepare the meal. The soft drink bottler would provide drinks at cost.

"I think we're okay," said Ed, "though I'm hoping to scare up another server on the lunch line."

"Get two," advised Adam. "You'll always have a no-show, and if another one gets sick, you're in big trouble. How's the program coming?"

"Fine," said Ceil. "The layout's done, the printer's been warned it'll be a rush job, and I'm just waiting another day because Milt said he's FedExing his photo to me." The program was printed as late as possible in order to include as many entries as possible. It came in the form of a magazine, and each entry was to supply a color photograph of his or her vehicle. Onlookers enjoyed being able to look up and identify a car they had seen and liked.

"Did we take Bill Birmingham's name off the program?" Adam asked, and there was an awkward shuffle.

Ceil said, "That's something we should discuss. Some of us think we should leave it, maybe put a black border around it." Bill's photo showed him at last year's run, the first one he and Charlotte drove in the 1910 Maxwell. The photo had been taken in New London, with the two of them aboard looking happy and confident. The look had vanished by the halfway point, when they'd staggered into Buffalo two hours late. Their car had not been able to continue.

"What will Charlotte think when she sees it?" Adam asked.

"She's not coming," Ceil said. "I talked with her this morning and she told me to tell you not to expect her."

"When's the funeral?" asked Henry.

Ceil replied, "They don't know yet. The medical examiner hasn't released the body."

There was a moment's silence, then Ed remarked, "This whole business sucks. I don't know which aspect sucks the worst, but there isn't an aspect that doesn't."

"I call the question," said Henry, who was familiar with Robert's Rules of Order.

"What does that mean?" asked Adam, who wasn't.

"That means, let's vote on the motion."

"Nobody made a motion," noted Ceil.

"All right, I move we leave Bill's name and photo in the program, with a black border."

"Second," said Mike.

The motion carried five to two, Henry and Adam being the two dissenters. Henry thought they should either make a big fuss, dedicate the run to Bill, ask for a moment of silence and put a big picture on the first page of the program—or drop the photo out of the program and say nothing at all. Though no one wanted to say so now, Bill hadn't been popular enough for the first to have any meaning, so Henry voted for the second. Adam thought it would make people who knew the ugly details of Bill's death uncomfortable to find him beaming out at them from the program, even with a black border. He knew it would him. So he voted against it.

Early in the afternoon a woman came into Crewel World. Betsy didn't recognize her. She was in her late twenties, too thin, with fine-grained skin lightly touched with freckles, dark blond hair pulled carelessly back into a scrunchie, and a sleeveless, pale pink dress a size too large. She looked around with an experienced eye, then went to the racks of counted patterns. After a few minutes, she picked up a black-on-white pattern called A Twinkling of Trees and brought it to the desk.

"What do you recommend for the fabric for this?" she asked. Her light blue eyes would have been her best feature if she had thought to use a touch of mascara on her very pale eyelashes.

"I'm doing it on Aida," said Betsy. "I should warn you it's almost all backstitching," she added, because many stitchers become very cross about backstitching.

"I can see that, but there's something primal about trees standing in snow, don't you think? Plus it reminds me of where I grew up. We don't get a lot of snow where I live now."

"Are you from Minnesota?"

"Oh, yes, I'm Lisa Birmingham." But not for long, to judge by the three-carat engagement diamond on a long, slender finger. Well, unless she decided to keep her name, thought Betsy. Which she might, because this was *Dr.* Lisa Birmingham, the pediatrician.

"How do you do?" said Betsy. "I'm Betsy Devonshire. I'm so sorry about your father."

"Yes, well, that's the real reason I'm here. You spoke with my mother yesterday. Has my brother been to see you as well?"

"Yes, a little while ago."

"Well, I'm sure he tried to warn you off."

"Yes, he did."

She leaned forward and said with quiet intensity, "Ignore him. Help my mother. She's going crazy, and the police won't leave her alone."

"You don't think the police suspect her?"

"Yes, I do, though I don't see how. But I want as many people as possible working on solving this. The more people trying, the better, don't you agree?"

"Possibly. Your brother seems to think I'll do something that will spoil the investigation."

"Will you?"

"Not if I can help it."

"Well, then. Do your darndest to help us, won't you?"

"All right. Have you got a few minutes to talk with me?"

"What for, what about?"

"Your father, your brother, anything you think might help."

"All right. But I live in St. Louis, and have for three years. I don't get home very often. So I don't know if I'll be much help."

Betsy led her to the back of the shop, where two cozy upholstered chairs faced one another across a small, round table. "Here, have a seat," she invited the woman. "Would you like a cup of coffee, or tea?"

"Coffee, black, thanks."

Betsy brought her the coffee in a small, pretty porcelain cup, and for herself a cup of green tea. Each took a polite sip. Betsy said, "How much older than you is Broward?"

"Three years. Bro is the oldest, then there's me, then Tommy is not quite three years younger, and David is two years younger than Tommy. I assume Mother bragged about us?"

"Yes, of course. She said Broward quit an excellent job to go into business with his father, that you are a pediatrician, Tommy owns a car dealership, and David is going for an advanced degree in education."

Lisa nodded, smiling. "I see she's still prouder of my M.D. license than my engagement to Mark. You have a good memory."

"I was interested. Your mother has good reason to be proud of her children. But tell me, how did your father persuade Broward to give up a position with a bigger company and come to work for him?"

"That wasn't the way it was supposed to be. My father was supposed to retire and let Bro take over the business. Father's doctor warned him years ago that he had to retire and start taking it easy. Father chose not to believe him. His blood pressure was high and he said medications prescribed for him weren't working, though what I think was, he wasn't taking them. They make you sleepy, you know, and he couldn't stand that. So he'd take them for a couple of days before he was supposed to go have his pressure checked, and that wasn't always long enough. Drove his doctor crazy until he finally figured out what Dad was doing. And meanwhile Father refused to work fewer hours.

"Then he had a ministroke, and that scared him. He phoned Bro and told him he was ready to retire, and did Bro want to take over the company. Bro said sure— he wasn't moving up fast enough in the company he was working for.

"But Father couldn't quit, not completely. At first he said he had to show Bro the ropes, then he said he wanted to see how Bro was doing, and finally he said he just couldn't trust Bro to run the company the way it should be run."

"Bill's way," said Betsy.

"That's right. Bro had his own ideas, and Father couldn't allow that."

Betsy took another sip of her tea and said, "How angry was Bro at his father?"

Lisa thought a moment and said, "Not murderously angry, of course. He could have quit, gone back to being a production manager at his former company—they want him back, they write him letters asking him to come back—and he told me he was thinking about going back to wait for Father to die."

"Was that likely to have happened soon? I mean, do you know how dangerously ill your father was?"

"Last time I talked to Mother, before all this happened, she said the doctor told her that Father would have a serious stroke within six months if he didn't slow down."

"Did Bro know this?"

"I don't know. I think so. If Mother told me, she probably told Bro, Tommy, and David, too."

"Was your father supposed to give up the cars, too?"

"Oh, no. They were a hobby. I'm reasonably sure it never occurred to anyone to tell the doctor that he worked as hard on those cars as he did at running his company."

"Did you know he was thinking about starting a company to supply parts to antique car collectors?"

Lisa sighed. "No, but that sounds a lot like Father."

"Do you have any idea how valuable his antique cars are?"

"The Maxwells are fairly common. Mother will probably get the best price for the Fuller. That's a really rare car."

"Fuller? I thought all your father collected were Maxwells."

"He did, except he bought this one Fuller. It's a Nebraska Fuller, not a Michigan, a high wheeler from 1910."

Betsy hadn't been this confused since she first worked in Crewel World and someone asked her if DMC 312 could be substituted for Paternayan 552. Betsy hadn't even known the customer was talking about embroidery floss. "High wheeler?" she repeated now, in the same tone that she'd echoed, "Paternayan?"

"Oh!" said Lisa. "I thought since you volunteered to work on the Antique Car Run that you knew something about these old cars."

"Well, I don't. What's a high wheeler?"

"The wheels are bigger in circumference, like buggy wheels. Automobile wheels are smaller. I think Father bought the Fuller because Adam wanted it."

"Do you mean Adam Smith?"

"Yes. He and Father were kind of rivals. You know how they keep saying, 'This isn't a race, the run isn't a race'?"

Betsy nodded.

"Well, not everyone believes that. And whenever Adam beat one of Father's Maxwells in one of his frail old rarities, Father was fit to be tied. Adam collects rarities and he wanted that Fuller very badly. Father bought it mostly to annoy him."

"And partly because—?"

"Oh, once Father was sure Adam had given up trying to get it, he was going to sell it at a profit. He'd already had a couple of bids on it from other collectors."

"So this wasn't a friendly rivalry."

Lisa hesitated, then decided candor was necessary. "At first it was. Then Adam bought a 1910 Maxwell that Father wanted badly. His plan was to resell it to Father at a nice profit. But Father, just to spite him, bought a different 1910 Maxwell—and it turned out to be a cantankerous machine, always something wrong with it. So Father was doubly angry with Adam. I think Adam was feeling guilty about the trick, but then Father bought the Fuller and wouldn't sell it to Adam at any price. Adam was furious."

"Couldn't they have gotten together on some kind of trade, maybe with cash added to make it even? I assume the Fuller was worth quite a bit more than the Maxwell."

"Yes, quite a bit, but neither was willing to talk to the other. In fact, Mother told me that the last time Adam and Father's paths crossed, Adam told Father that he was looking forward to Father's death, so he could come to the estate sale and buy that Fuller." She looked at her watch and jumped to her feet. "I'm supposed to take Mother to the lawyer's office, and I'll be late if I don't leave right now." She plunged her hand into her small white purse and pulled out a card. "Are you on the Internet?"

"Yes."

"Good. This has my e-mail address on it, contact me that way if you have any more questions. If Bro finds out I'm talking to you, he'll be angry, so I'd better not come out here anymore. And you can't call me. With everyone at home, e-mail's the only way to guarantee a private conversation. Bye." She grabbed up her purchases and left. Since they had been put into a Crewel World plastic drawstring bag, it was likely at least some of the family knew where she had been. This would serve as a reason why. But the metro area was scattered with needlework shops, most of them closer to Roseville than Crewel World, so most would quickly figure out why Lisa found it necessary to travel all the way out here to buy a cross stitch pattern.

Betsy rinsed the cups and went out front to assist a customer who came in to buy the threads for a pattern she'd found at a garage sale. Betsy managed to find all but one, which had been given the unhelpful name "Dawn's Favorite." But by consulting the pattern and locating where the unknown color was to be used, then looking at the colors around it, she realized it must be a shade of pink not already selected. She pulled three related shades from a spinner rack and, by giving the customer her choice, made her a collaborator and less likely to decide later she was unsatisfied with the color.

"Did Lisa help you decide Broward is a murderer?" asked Godwin when the customer was gone.

"No. In fact, she gave me a new suspect, Adam Smith."

"I thought you liked Adam Smith."

"I do. But it's a shame how many nice people commit murder."

10

The shop was closed, but Betsy remained, restoring order to the sale bins, restocking spinner racks, washing coffee cups. Saving the best for last, she opened a box containing an order of twelve clear glass Christmas tree ornaments. She was making a small display of them on a shelf in the back area when someone knocked on the front door.

It was Jill, bent over so the night light fell on her face as she peered around the needlepointed Closed sign. She was wearing a very pale yellow blouse and tan capri pants.

Betsy unlocked the door, and Jill said, "I rang the bell to your apartment but there was no answer so I decided to see if you were in here."

"Is something wrong?" asked Betsy.

"No, I have the night off, Lars is doing something

strange to his Stanley, and I just wanted to talk. Mind?"

"Not at all. Come in," said Betsy. "I'm working in back." Jill went on through the opening between the high stacks of box shelves, into the counted cross stitch section, while Betsy relocked the door and reset the alarm.

Betsy had turned off the ceiling lights in back, turning the many models hung on the walls into angled shadows.

"Whatcha doin' with those?" Jill asked when she saw the ornaments. "Isn't it kind of early for Christmas?"

Betsy said, "RCTN gave me the idea. You take these plain ornaments and fill them with orts." *Ort* is a crossword-puzzle word whose dictionary meaning is "morsel, as of food." But RCTN, the Internet news group of needleworkers, had adapted it to mean the little ends of floss or thread left over from stitching. Most threw orts away, but some collected them, filling old glass jars with the tiny fragments and displaying them. Betsy had seen the ornaments at an after-Christmas sale, and had bought one to fill with her own orts. Long before it was filled, she saw how beautiful it was going to be, and was sorry she hadn't bought more to sell in the shop. Then a few weeks ago she'd seen the ornaments in a catalog and ordered a dozen.

Now, she picked up her ort-filled ornament and handed it to Jill. "What do you think?"

"Say, this is *nice*! What a great idea! How much is one?"

"Empty, three dollars. I haven't set a price for filled yet."

"Who wants one full of someone else's leavings? It'll be fun filling it with my own. In fact, I'll take two."

Pleased at this early evidence of a success, Betsy said, "I'll put them aside for you—my cash register's closed for the night. Have you had supper yet?"

"No, I was going to ask if you wanted to go halves on a pizza."

"I'd rather have Chinese."

"But I was thinking of eating at home—yours or mine. Like I said, I want to talk to you."

"Is this about Lars thinking of buying another Stanley Steamer?"

Jill stared at Betsy.

"I take it he didn't tell you."

"No." Jill could be very terse when annoyed.

"He said the later models had condensers on them so he wouldn't have to stop every twenty-five miles to take on water."

"I see."

"I told him to consult you before he bought one."

"Thank you."

"Chinese take-out, then?"

"Fine."

"I'll buy if you'll fly."

"Okay."

Excelsior had its own Chinese restaurant, the Ming Wok, just a few blocks away. By the time Jill came back with the warm, white paper sack emitting delectable smells, Betsy had finished in the shop and was up in her apartment.

And Jill was over her mad.

They sat down to feast on Mongolian beef and chicken with pea pods.

Jill, feeling the cat Sophie's gentle pressure on her foot, dropped one hand carelessly downward, an ort of chicken even more carelessly hanging from her fingers. Sophie deftly removed it and Jill brought her hand back up to the table to wipe it on a napkin.

"If you leave your hand down there, she'll lick it clean and I'll be less likely to notice you wiping your fingers and guess what you're up to," said Betsy.

Jill laughed. "I'll remember that. But since you didn't jump up and shout at Sophie, or me, I take it you no longer disapprove. So why don't you just give up and feed her, too?"

"I do feed her. She gets Iams Less Active morning and evening. She gets enough to maintain a cat at sixteen pounds, which is what she'd weigh pretty soon if everyone else would just stop sneaking her little treats."

"I mean—"

"I know what you mean. Jill, you stayed here last December, and you saw what she's like when feeding time approaches, whining and pacing and driving me crazy. That's what she'd be like every time I sat down at this table if she thought I allowed her to have something from my plate. So long as she thinks I forbid it, she's content to be slipped a treat on the sly by someone else, and she's very quiet about it. So I do my part, scolding her—and you and everyone else—when it gets too blatant. Look at her."

Jill looked down then around and saw Sophie all the way across the living room, curled into her cushioned basket. She looked back with mild, innocent surprise at their regard. "See that smirk? She thinks she's got me fooled. Help me maintain the fiction, all right?"

Jill raised a solemn right hand. "I promise." She opened her fortune cookie. "Mine says, *Tomorrow is your lucky day.* Always tomorrow, never today. What does yours say?"

Betsy opened hers. *"The solution lies within your grasp,"* she read. "To what, I wonder?"

Jill said, with a little smile, "How about the Birmingham murder? How's that coming?"

"Not very well. I don't know the people, I don't know enough about antique cars, I don't know as much about the actual scene of the crime. And you can't really help this time because the Excelsior police aren't investigating."

"Well," drawled Jill, "it just so happens I have prints of photos taken at the Highway 5 lay-by."

Betsy said, "That's what you came to talk about, isn't it? You came here meaning to show them to me."

"Only if the subject came up. Which it was going to. Where's my purse?" She looked around, saw it in the living room, and stood. "Come on, have a look."

But a minute later, pulling a brown envelope out, she hesitated. "Um, these aren't pretty."

Betsy hesitated, too. She was not fond of the uglier details. "Well, let's see how bad they are."

They were awful. Betsy hastily took several close-ups of the head of the victim off the top of the stack, putting them facedown on the coffee table. The next one was of the horribly burned upper body, and she pulled it off, too. "How do the people who deal with this sort of thing stand it?" she asked.

"By making horrible jokes." Betsy looked up at Jill, who was standing beside the upholstered chair Betsy was sitting on. "I'm serious," she continued. "They call burn victims crispy critters, for example. They have to; otherwise, they'd be so sick they couldn't conduct a proper investigation." She shrugged at Betsy's appalled expression. "You asked."

Betsy returned her attention to the photographs. The next few were of the burned-out Maxwell. "The whole inside seems to be gone," she noted.

"Yes, and it smelled of accelerant."

"Accelerant?"

"Something combustible, like gasoline or kerosene. Which at first wasn't suspicious, because after all a car uses gasoline. But some of the ash they collected from the back seat contained gasoline."

Betsy looked at the photo again. "How could there be any accelerant left in something this thoroughly burned?"

"Because it isn't liquid gasoline that burns, it's the vapor. You can actually put a match out by sticking it into a bucket of gasoline—unless it's been sitting long enough for fumes to gather, in which case the fumes will explode as your lit match enters the cloud. Arsonists who spend too long splashing accelerant around are arrested when they go to the emergency room with burns."

"You know the doggondest things."

"I know. Look at the rest of the photos, and see if there's anything to see." She had taken out a notebook and pen, prepared to write down anything interesting Betsy might notice.

Betsy obediently looked. Since she knew very little about automobiles and even less about antique ones, the photos of the burnt-out car told her nothing. She noted the hammer in the puddle of dirty water around the car and remembered the joke hollered by a fellow driver last Saturday: Get a bigger hammer!

She asked Jill, "Do you know if they found evidence Bill was struck on the head before being shot?"

"Not that I know of. Why would someone do that?"

"Maybe it was a quarrel he had with someone and he got hit in the head with that hammer. Or maybe he swung it at someone, who pulled a gun and shot him. I understand he was a very aggressive type."

"Hmmm," said Jill, writing that down.

Farther down were more photos of the corpse. Again Betsy hurried past them, but she slowed at several taken of just the lower portion of the body, which was barely damaged. The white flannel trousers were barely smudged, and then only above the knees. Except . . .

"What?" asked Jill.

Betsy looked closer, frowning. "That's funny, that smudge right there looks more like someone wiped his dirty fingers than smoke or fire damage."

"Let me see." Jill took the photo and peered at it closely. "Where's your Dazor?"

"In the guest bedroom."

"Bring it here, will you?" She spoke peremptorily, slipping into cop mode without thinking.

Betsy went into the bedroom her sister had used and opened the closet to pull out the wheeled stand with the gooseneck lamp on it. She wheeled it out into the living room and plugged it in.

Jill turned on the full-spectrum fluorescent light that encircled the rectangular magnifying glass and bent the gooseneck to a convenient angle to view the photo. "Huh," she said after half a minute. "It does look like someone wiped dust off his fingers, it's so faint . . ."

Betsy took the photo and held it under the magnifier.

"Maybe it's an old stain that didn't wash out. Funny I didn't notice it Saturday."

"Why funny?"

"Well, I do remember noticing how immaculately white they were. No, wait, he had a towel tucked into his belt to keep the grease off, so it would have covered these old stains up. Oh, and here's—no."

"No, what?"

"Not flecks of dirt, orts."

"Where?"

"On his trousers, near the cuffs. Charlotte really could use one of those glass ornaments, she sprinkles orts wherever she goes. Her daughter Lisa came into the shop on Monday and I said I knew she was a stitcher when I saw the orts on her dress and she said they were her mother's—though I was right about Lisa being a stitcher. Her mother is a nice, nice woman, but even I came home Saturday with some of her orts on my clothes. She kind of flicks them off the ends of her fingers." Betsy looked again at the photo. She could not have said why she found the few tiny ends of floss clinging to Bill's trousers so touching.

She gave the photos back to Jill and said, "I assume the police have the same two suspects I have. Do you know if they have more than two?"

"Our department is only marginally involved, so I'm not sure how many suspects Steffans at Minnetonka PD has. I hear he'd love Charlotte for this, but you gave her a terrific alibi."

"He'd love her why, because they always look at the spouse?"

"That's part of it. The other part is, they're getting reports that the couple weren't getting along, hadn't been getting along for the past several years."

Betsy said, "Charlotte told me they were in counseling, and things were starting to turn around. Certainly she seemed affectionate toward Bill when I saw them."

"Seriously affectionate or polite affectionate?"

"She patted him on the rump when she went to tell him she was riding with me to St. Paul."

"If she was feeling so chummy, why didn't she ride with him?"

"Because he was having trouble with the car, and she said it was jiggling so unevenly it was making her sick." Betsy frowned. "Is that likely? I've never ridden in an old car other than Lars's, and that old steamer has a very smooth way of going."

"Lars told me that was a selling point, that the internal combustion cars of that period did jiggle. He says it was a combination of too few cylinders and no shock absorbers."

Betsy nodded. "In Charlotte's case, there may also have been the prospect of having to sit in the hot sun wearing all those clothes while Bill worked on it after it broke down on the road—I mean, he had trouble starting it, and when he did, it was still idling rough, so she probably guessed it was going to break down. Which apparently it did. He spent the whole time they were in Excelsior with his head under the hood."

"So if not Charlotte, who are your suspects?"

"I hardly dare say they're actual suspects, but the two I'd like to know more about are Bill's son Broward and Adam Smith."

"Who's Adam Smith?"

"He was in charge of Saturday's run," Betsy said. She explained about the ongoing quarrel between him and Bill, concluding, "I don't know how powerful a motive that is, but I do know Charlotte and I waited quite a long time for Adam to show up in St. Paul."

"Who could you ask, do you know?"

"Not offhand, not anyone who wouldn't go right to Adam and tell him I'm asking questions. He's president of the Antique Car Club, and from the little I've seen, he seems to be very popular." Betsy had gone to exactly one meeting of the Antique Car Club with Lars, just to see if it was something she wanted to get more deeply involved with. It had been interesting—but also obvious that this was one of those organizations that ate up all a member's spare time, and Betsy didn't feel she wanted to spend what little spare time she had on this organization. After all, she was not going to buy an antique car of her own. She told Lars on the way home that she would volunteer for this year's run, because Lars was a part of it and she was Lars's sponsor, but after that, he was on his own.

"Are you afraid that if he did it and thinks you're closing in on him, he might come after you?"

"Oh, nothing like that," Betsy said. "I don't want to get people all stirred up about my thinking it might be Adam, when I really think he's only a possibility. Being suspected of murder can ruin someone, even if it turns out he didn't do it. If I knew more about antique car owners or the Antique Car Club, I might form a real opinion. Why do people collect them and how fanatical do they get about them? Adam would have to be totally invested in getting that Fuller to consider murdering Bill."

Jill said, "They're probably like every other set of hobbyists. Some are casual, some are intent, some are fanatical. You talked with Adam, which kind is he?"

Betsy remembered Ceil's jeer at Adam's remark that he might be willing to find a buyer for Joe Mickels's McIntyre. "As if you'd let anyone else get their hands on it!" she'd said, or words to that effect.

But Betsy was unwilling to say anything out loud, even to Jill.

Godwin was in Shelly's kitchen, doing the dishes, when the phone rang. "I'll get it!" he caroled, wiping his hands on his apron. He lifted the receiver on the wall near the back door. "Hello?"

"Goddy?" said a man's voice in a near-whisper.

"Who is this?" said Godwin, though he knew.

"Don't be stupid, for heaven's sake!"

"Why, hello, John," drawled Godwin in as dry a voice as he could manage, though his heart was already singing.

"I'm concerned that I haven't heard from you."

"Well, you made it pretty clear—twice—that you didn't want anything to do with me ever again."

"I was angry. You made me very angry. Sometimes, Goddy, when you act like you don't care about me, I just can't stand it."

"You suspected I didn't care about you, so you stopped caring about me."

"I have never stopped caring about you. Ever. Even when I'm angry—even in a jealous rage. Goddy, sometimes you exasperate me beyond endurance. You know you do. You know you're doing it when it happens."

"I wasn't doing anything you could get mad about."

"Goddy, I *saw* you talking to—"

Godwin hung up at that point with a satisfied little smile.

11

Wednesday morning Betsy's alarm went off at 5:15. Sophie, who had been rescued from the street many years ago, retained a fear of abandonment. She became very much underfoot and vocal at this change in routine. Betsy reassured her, "Come on, I've been doing this for a week," though it had been only three days a week, not enough to have sunk into Sophie's unsophisticated brain.

Betsy put on an old swimsuit, over which she put a good linen-blend dress in a shade of pale rose and matching sandals, her going-to-work outfit. She packed underwear, shampoo, soap, and a towel in a light zippered bag and, ignoring Sophie's anxious inquiries about breakfast, went down to the back door and out. She was going exercising.

Betsy had been meaning to take up horseback riding

or maybe power walking, but with running her shop, trying to learn enough about roof repair to choose a roofer for her building, dealing with her tenants, volunteering with the Antique Car Run, and keeping up with household chores, she just hadn't managed to add an exercise program.

She did manage a couple of hours for a physical a few weeks ago, and her doctor said she would have more energy if she would stop writing IOUs to her body and find some kind of exercise she would actually do. So Betsy investigated and found an early-bird water aerobics program that met three mornings a week. Betsy chose it partly because of all forms of exercise this was the least distasteful, but mostly because she didn't have to carve a couple of hours out of her working day, an impossible task. This flock of early birds met at 6:30 A.M. for an hour. Betsy would be back in her apartment by 8:30, showered, dressed, and on time for her pre-exercise routine: her and Sophie's breakfast, e-mail, a bit of bookkeeping or bill paying, and down in the shop by 10:00.

But first she had to get there. Oddly enough, at 5:45 in the morning, the rush hour into the Cities was swift enough to deserve the name. Betsy drove toward Minneapolis, but only as far as Golden Valley. She exited onto Highway 100, then took Golden Valley Drive to The Courage Center, a brick building in its own small valley, parked in the nearly empty lot, and went in. All three women behind the big reception counter were in wheelchairs. The Courage Center's primary aim was to restore injured bodies to health and bring handicapped bodies to their full potential—hence its name, and the status of its employees—but it also offered pool exercise to all comers.

In the women's locker room four other women greeted Betsy with that muted cheer found before 6:30 A.M. All were at least middle-aged. More women came in until they were eight and they all, after perfunctory showers, trailed down a short hallway to a large room nearly full of an enormous swimming pool. Between pillars on the far wall large panes of glass were hung, with stained glass sections making a thinly traced and almost abstract map showing a confluence of rivers.

The water was warm. The pool, instead of sloping from shallow to deep, had four large flat areas, each a foot or so deeper than the one before. The shallowest area was three and a half feet deep, and Betsy went there with three of the other women to start walking back and forth. Two men joined them. Disco music began to play. A cheerful and energetic young woman in a professional swimsuit came to stand in the water and direct the movements.

"Good morning, Jodie," said several of the more-awake women. This did not include Betsy, who could not even remember Jodie's name, though it had been Jodie who had interviewed Betsy just last week while signing up for this program.

"Let's keep walking, knees high," called Jodie, standing waist deep in the pool. She was taller than Betsy, on whom the water came nearly to her armpits.

After a few minutes of this, Betsy's brain sputtered to life. "Hi, Florence, hi, Ruth, hi, Barbara," she said, pushing her way through the water past them, knees high and glutes tight. She had a lot of catching up to do.

A few minutes later, they were sidestepping, bending

sideways, and reaching with the lead arm, when Florence, at eighty the most senior person present, said as Betsy flowed past her, "Look, Betsy, we have a new person here today." Florence nodded toward one of the deeper areas, and Betsy looked over. And stopped dead in the water.

"Why, I know her, that's Charlotte Birmingham!"

"No, not Charlotte," said Florence impatiently. "She's been coming for a long time. I mean the man."

"But I don't remember seeing Charlotte here before," said Betsy.

"She sometimes stops coming for a week or so. She travels, I think."

"Oh." Of course. Charlotte had been getting ready for last week's run. Betsy thought about going deeper to say hello, then decided against it. She was getting into this sidestepping business, feeling the push of water against her legs and *reeeeaching*, feeling the good stretch. In a while everyone would climb aboard a Styrofoam "noodle" and go paddling out into the deepest water. She'd say hello then.

"Jumping jacks with elbow kisses, side to side!" called Jodie, and everyone continued moving sideways but now in jumping jack motions, bringing elbows together in front and out again. There was no way Betsy could have done this for this long on dry land, but with the lift and support of the water, it was fun and not too difficult.

She looked again at the man, who was out beyond Charlotte, in the second-deepest area. He was taller than Charlotte, but not by a lot. He was trim and muscular, though he wasn't young. His hair, a light brown, showed no trace of gray—Grecian Formula, concluded

Betsy. He had a pleasant face, presently lit with laughter as he struggled with the unfamiliar movement. Charlotte, facing him and moving well, said something to him and his head went back as his laughter intensified.

"Find a place to cross-country ski!" called Jodie, and the swimmers settled into stationary places where they could swing their arms and move their legs without bumping or splashing one another. The man looked around to see how it was done, and set a rapid pace, churning the water with arm movements, grinning. Charlotte turned to face him, her expression a mirror of his.

Betsy was surprised, then surprised at her surprise. The man was enjoying himself, why shouldn't Charlotte? Then she realized Charlotte's face held the same warm, open look of amused affection she'd had last Saturday. Only then it had been directed at her husband.

"So she was having a good time," said Godwin when Betsy told him about it. "I've heard it's possible for people to enjoy doing more than one thing. Who is he, anyone we know?"

Betsy was going through her half-price-floss basket, pulling out items that were starting to look shopworn. She'd use them to make up more kits. "I don't think so. I wonder if he's another antique car buff. I talked to Charlotte in the locker room, but only briefly because we both had to get going. She said the man's name is Marvin Pierce, a business associate of Bill's who became friends with both of them, and now he's rallied round the whole family, running errands and being a general help."

"So what's the problem?"

"I'm probably making something out of nothing, but she seemed so . . . cheerful with him. She wasn't acting like a new widow and he wasn't acting like a comfort to the bereaved. It was startling to see her laughing and having a good time."

"Well, you can't cry twenty-four hours a day, can you? And she told you this guy's been really helping out. So she laughed for an hour because he made her forget." A thought struck. "You say she didn't introduce you in the pool. You think that was on purpose?"

"No. I went over to Charlotte and we exchanged hellos, and she said I was going to love this program, she's been doing it for years. Then Barbara noodled over to ask me where my shop was, and when I finished telling her and looked around, Charlotte was over talking with Ruth and Leah." Betsy frowned, trying to be sure there'd been nothing suspicious about her not getting introduced to Marvin. She would have introduced herself, but Marvin had gone to share a joke with Joe and she hadn't wanted to intrude.

"You can't be thinking she did it," said Godwin.

"No, of course not, I know that's impossible. But I'm thinking how she told me that she'd been going to a counselor and things had been improving between her and her husband. But she said he wouldn't go with her, and I've heard that both have to go before you can turn a marriage around. So suppose things weren't actually improving? And suppose she turned to an old friend for advice and comfort?"

"You mean this Marvin fellow."

"Yes. And suppose that old friend and she decided the best form of help involved killing Bill? Maybe it was a plot the two of them cooked up, because then, you see, she would have a very good reason to get close to someone on that Saturday, and stick with that someone, who could give her an unbreakable alibi."

"Does this Marvin fellow drive an antique car?"

"I don't know. But he didn't need to, really. All he had to do was sabotage the Maxwell's engine and watch for Bill to pull over."

Godwin said admiringly, "How your mind works! That's a wickedly clever plot—too bad for whoever did it that you're even cleverer! But how can you prove it? I mean you can't find out if the Maxwell was sabotaged, because it's all burned up. And who did it?"

"I don't know, but he took an awful chance, burning the Maxwell. The police are very clever nowadays proving arson. Or is it the fire department that investigates suspicious fires? Whichever, they thought the fire was suspicious from the start."

"Not so clever, then."

"And you know, I may be wrong about all this. It's just one of several possibilities." Betsy remembered again that look of affection Charlotte had given her husband, the gentle caress she gave as she left him to his frantic car repairing on Saturday. It had seemed spontaneous, authentic. She said, "I haven't had a chance to look into Adam Smith's drive from Excelsior to St. Paul, for example." She checked her watch. "Time to open up," she said.

Godwin went to turn the needlepoint sign so OPEN faced outward, and realized someone was waiting for the door to be unlocked.

It was Irene. "Hello, hello, hello!" she caroled, striding into the shop with a broad, happy smile. Betsy and Godwin exchanged a surprised glance. Neither had ever seen her wholly joyous like this, without a hint of anxiety or arrogance. "Have you got a shopping basket?" she asked.

Godwin grasped the situation faster than Betsy. "Big or small?" he asked, reaching for a two-gallon size currently holding yarn and nodding at the pint-size one Betsy was taking floss out of.

"Oh, the big one," said Irene, and Godwin happily spilled its yarn onto the library table, then handed it to her.

Godwin said to Betsy, "Some people go to Disney World, Irene comes here."

Irene chortled in agreement and began to fill the basket. Never in her life had she been able to buy as much as she wanted of ribbon, floss, wool yarn, silk yarn, alpaca yarn, and fabric, in every desirable color, all at one time, with no thought of the cost. Irene filled the basket three times. Betsy, eyeing the heap, estimated there was over a thousand dollars' worth, and Irene had not bought a single painted canvas—the most expensive single item a needleworker can buy.

"Have you quit your job yet?" teased Godwin, helping Betsy start to write up the order.

Irene said, "No, but I'm thinking about it. What do you think, Betsy?"

Betsy said, "I think you shouldn't, not yet. You'll lose your benefits when you do, and I know from experience how expensive buying your own medical insurance is. Right now you need to talk to a financial advisor, which all by itself is going to cost you something."

"Oh," said Irene, the light in her eyes dimming just a little.

"I'm sorry to let more air out of your balloon," said Betsy, "and much as I would like to encourage you to continue buying one or two of everything in my shop, I think you should be aware that you are going to have to share any money you received with the state and federal government."

"Maybe I should put some of this back," said Irene, now definitely looking alarmed.

But Godwin said, "Oh, come on, it's not as bad as all that. How much did you take in last weekend?" asked Godwin.

She turned to him. "Twenty-seven thousand."

Godwin whistled.

"But I had to give fifteen percent of that to the gallery. On the other hand, I have orders for two more pieces, and Mark—Mr. Duggan—wants me to bring in three more by the end of the month. That's why I was thinking of quitting, because I can't think how I can do all that in so short a time. These pieces take a lot of planning, and they're complicated to stitch. Also, a reporter from the *Star Tribune* interviewed me and they took pictures. After that appears in next week's *Variety* section, there's likely to be even more orders."

"Then for heaven's sake, don't worry about spending a single thousand here! What are you charging for these orders?"

"Depends. The most expensive is five thousand. One of the orders is for a small piece, and I'm asking twenty-two hundred for it. It's only six inches by six inches. Is that too much?"

"On the contrary. Raise your prices."

"But I'm already charging so much—"

"You can't fill the orders you're getting now. Raise

your prices until you have only as many orders as you can fill. I bet you could charge twenty or thirty thousand apiece and still have enough work to keep you busy." He glanced at Betsy. "*And* buy medical insurance. What you'll have left over even after you pay those nasty taxes will keep you very comfortably."

Involuntarily, Irene's hand reached out as if to touch Godwin on his hand, but stopped before she made contact. She turned to Betsy. "Could he possibly be right?"

"He might be. He knows a lot about things like this. Maybe you also need to hire an agent."

"Oh my, oh my, oh my," Irene murmured. The glow had come back. "An *agent*."

Godwin said, in a darker voice, "So long as you're listening to me, hear this: Art is the strangest thing. What you're doing may grow and grow, or it may vanish entirely overnight. It's like, one year the museums can't get enough big piles of penny candy, the next year it's Lent."

"What I do isn't silly like those piles of candy!" flared Irene. "What I do is real work!"

"Oh, I agree," said Godwin quickly. "It's a form of Impressionism, which has been around for a long time and is a very respected art form. But the quote real unquote Impressionists use paint on canvas. It may be the critics will decide you're just as real in this different medium. Or they may decide it's a weird offshoot, a cute fad, but not really valid."

Irene glared at him, panting, yearning to fight, but she was weaponless.

"Do you have some vacation time coming?" asked Betsy, anxious to sooth her savage breast.

"What? Oh, yes, I haven't taken any yet this year, and I get three weeks."

"You might see if you can take some now to get a running start on these commissioned pieces."

"Now that's a good idea! And I will also seek professional advice." She smiled. "I am so glad I came in here to buy my materials!"

"So are we," said Godwin, smiling as he added his sales slips to the stack Betsy was adding up on her little calculator. "So are we."

12

On Wednesday, her hair still damp despite riding home from Courage Center with the windows down—she would never get used to the humidity around here—Betsy sat down at her computer to download her e-mail, going to make a second cup of tea while RCTN downloaded. There were always lots and lots of messages from the newsgroup, and there was generally a useful nugget or two among them. Betsy quickly arrowed down the subject lines, read several, replied to a few, then deleted the download.

Among her e-mail messages was one from Susan Greening Davis about window displays, a response to a question from Betsy—and another from Lisa Birmingham in reply to Betsy's e-mail of yesterday evening.

Lisa said she had long suspected her parents' marriage was "under a strain," but hadn't known about the counseling sessions. She was not surprised her father had refused to go. *My father never thought anyone else's opinion was superior to his own*, she wrote.

> *Did you get to talk with Marvin at The Courage Center pool? Isn't he a dear? I know it's far too early, but maybe in a year or two, Mother will stop seeing Marvin as the family's good friend and develop a romantic interest. I think he's in love with her. I think he's been in love with her for years. But he never even flirted with her, so far as I know. I remember when he came with my family to see me get my baccalaureate degree. Mother and Father were simply beaming at me, and a little off to the side I saw Marvin. He was looking at Mother. There was just that something in his eyes, you know what I mean. And I saw him look at her that way again when I was home last Christmas and she was opening his gift. He gave her an inexpensive piece of antique jet jewelry. She gave him a gag gift, a pair of socks in a shocking fuchsia color I think she knit herself. I mean, where on earth would you find socks that color in a man's size? He actually wore them to a New Year's Eve party at the Herbert Manleys the next week. He didn't care who saw the socks, and if that's not love, what is? But I asked Mother what she thought of Marvin not long ago and she said, "I'm so glad he's a friend of this family." She's a bit of an actress, but I'm sure she has no idea.*

Betsy clicked on Reply and typed, *You are very observant. Thank you. Now, can you find out where Bro-*

*ward and Marvin were on the day your father was
murdered?*

Lars never did anything by halves. Now that his new
hobby consisted of an old car, he researched it thoroughly, reading books and looking for web sites on the
Internet devoted to Stanley Steamers, and downloaded
diagrams of Stanley Steamer plumbing to study. He
joined an international organization of Stanley Steamer
owners. Once a Steamer came to live with him, he contacted two Steamer owners in Wisconsin with questions,
and drove to Eau Claire to watch and learn how to
maintain his vehicle.

Lars's Stanley was built in 1912, an era when twenty-
five miles an hour on the road was remarkable. But
F. E. and F. O. Stanley, identical twin speed demons,
looked ahead to a period when forty miles an hour sus-
tained road speed would be desirable, and built their car
for that foreseen time. And just as they refused to consider the assembly line, they refused to acknowledge
planned obsolescence. When someone ordered a
Steamer from their factory, he had to wait for it to be
built by hand—and then was expected never to replace
it. That's why, as late as the mid-1950s, pioneer Stanley
boilers were still in outdoor use, lifting, cutting and
grinding stone in a New England gravel pit.

Currently, having acquired some understanding of his
Stanley, Lars was in a mood to manipulate it. While he
wouldn't dream of taking his Stanley on the Interstate,
he did sometimes get out on the state and county highways, where forty miles an hour was slow. He wondered if there was some way to adjust the flame under
the boiler so fifty or even fifty-five miles per hour could

be attained without having to stop even more often for water.

So when Betsy stopped in to see him around midday on Thursday, he had the burner disassembled and was consulting his owner's manual for advice.

"Oh, no!" she said, and he looked around to see her standing dismayed in the doorway to his barn.

"What's the matter?" he asked, putting down the vaporizing coil and reaching for a towel to wipe his hands.

"That's what I was about to ask you," said Betsy. "How bad is it?"

"How bad is what?"

"Are you going to be able to repair it by Saturday?"

He grinned. "It doesn't need repair," he said, to her obvious relief. "I was trying to figure out how to get a bigger head of steam without having to stop even more often for water."

Betsy began to giggle. "You sound like Tim Taylor on 'Home Improvement': 'More power!' "

"No, I sound like the Stanley twins that morning on Daytona Beach in 1907."

"Just be careful you don't become airborne. The run this weekend isn't a race, remember."

"I'll remember," he promised, without a hint that his fingers were crossed behind his back.

"So when are you going down to New London— tonight or Friday?"

"If I can figure out this burner business fast enough— or decide I can't figure it out soon enough—I thought I'd take 'er down this evening. Otherwise I'll leave here early in the morning. What, are you looking for a ride?"

"Oh, no, I'm leaving this evening after we close. I'm driving down. You do know a lot of drivers are already there, terrorizing the countryside with their infernal machines?"

Lars grinned. "I hear the populace turns out to wave as they go by. But I had to work yesterday."

"Do you have a motel reservation?"

"Naw, there's room for a bunk in the trailer, so I thought I'd camp out with it. It's only two nights. You?"

"I let it go too late. Every room in New London is taken, so I'm staying at the Lakeside Motel in Willmar, and commuting. But it's not far. So, I'll see you there. Oh, here's your sponsor's banner." Betsy handed over a twenty-four-by-ten-inch rectangle of plastic-coated canvas with the logo of her shop printed on it: CREWEL WORLD worked in X's as if it were cross stitched. On the corners were pockets holding powerful magnets, so Lars could put the banner anywhere on the vehicle he chose.

He took it, looked at it, then smiled shyly at her. "I want to thank you—" he began.

"It's all right, really," she interrupted hastily. "I was glad to do it." *Golly,* she thought on her way back to her shop, *I'm really turning into a Minnesotan, embarrassed to be thanked.*

The door went *Bing!* and Betsy came out from the back of her shop.

Charlotte stopped short when she saw Betsy. There was a tall man with her—Betsy suddenly realized it was Marvin Pierce, AKA Friend of the Family. "Oh, I thought you were in New London already," said Charlotte.

"No, I'm going up as soon as I close this evening. I had hoped to see you up there."

"No, no, I'm not going. The funeral has to be planned, though we still don't know which day that will be, the medical examiner hasn't, er, released Bill's body. Anyway, I couldn't face . . . those people. Not right now." Once the surprise drained away, her face showed the stress and sorrow of a new widow.

Marvin put a sympathetic hand on Charlotte's shoulder, and Betsy said, "Yes, of course, I understand. So what brings you out here?"

"I understand you have a very competent finisher."

"Yes, Heidi's wonderful. Do you have that Christie piece ready?"

"Yes." Charlotte came to the checkout desk and put a plastic bag on it. She opened it and lifted out a square wrapped in tissue paper.

Betsy came to unwrap it, saying, "You take such good care of your work. I had someone come in last week with a piece that looked as if she'd washed the car with it."

Marvin snorted his amused surprise. Charlotte said, "My regular finisher won't take a piece that's dirty."

"I can't afford to be very picky. I even have a woman who will go over pieces and fill in missing stitches, or repair torn or moth-eaten pieces. Sandy has rescued lots of heirloom pieces. But this looks perfect."

"It's as good as I can make it, and if there's some mistake in it, I don't want it fixed. This work is all mine. I found the original, photographed it, scanned it and made the pattern, and stitched it all by myself." She glanced up from it to meet Betsy's eyes and said, "Oh, all right, Grace Christie designed it, so it's essentially a copy. But I made some changes to her original pattern, worked some areas in different stitches from the original, and even altered the colors a little."

Marvin said, "She won't admit it, but I think what she does is equivalent to real art."

"Oh, tosh, Marvin," said Charlotte with a little frown.

Betsy's smile appeared. "Have you heard about Irene Potter?"

Charlotte said, "I read an article about her in one of our little weekly papers, yes. She stitches Impressionistic patterns, right?"

"Yes, but her first piece was almost a copy of a painting she admired. She did just about what you did, altered the pattern a little, changed some of the colors. So don't apologize."

Charlotte's spine straightened. "All right, I won't. I think this piece is great, and I'm proud of it."

"So you should be," said Marvin.

Betsy said, "I believe you wanted this made into a pillow?"

"Yes, that's right. But—well, can you give me an estimate of the cost?"

"Oh, never mind the cost," said Marvin. "If it's something you want, then go ahead and buy it."

"And who's going to pay for it?"

He looked at her, confused, and she looked away with a pained expression.

Betsy said, "Speaking from experience, it takes a long time to settle an estate. Things can get tight during that interim."

"Plus there are taxes and fees and all kinds of expenses," said Charlotte.

Marvin said, his voice showing he was still a little

puzzled, "I understand all that. But how much can it cost to get someone to sew this into a pillow? Twenty-five or thirty dollars?"

Betsy said to Charlotte, "He's not familiar with finishers, is he?"

Charlotte smiled. "No."

Betsy said to him, "I'm estimating this at about a hundred and fifty, minimum."

Marvin's eyebrows went high. He turned and looked around at the fibers, fabrics, and esoterica of needlework. "I had no idea. Cute little hobby you picked, Char." He turned back to show a very charming grin. "Of course, it isn't as pricey as antique cars."

Betsy said, "Do you own an antique car?"

"Whoa! Not me!" Marvin raised both hands. "I'd like to acquire some champagne tastes despite my beer budget, but not that one. What I like is for my cars to be as up to date as possible, with all the bells and whistles, thank you very much."

While Charlotte and Betsy became deeply involved in fabric selection, kinds of trim available, size, filler, and other considerations, Marvin went wandering around the shop. About twenty minutes later he was back at the desk.

Charlotte wrapped things up with Betsy, saying, "Use your best judgment, Betsy, but try to keep it under two hundred, all right?"

"Of course. How about I call you with Heidi's estimate before I tell her to go ahead?"

"Thank you." She turned and her eye was caught by a spinner rack of the newest in Watercolor flosses. She made as if to go to it, but instead said, "All right, all right, we can leave now," to Marvin, although he hadn't said a word.

Betsy's parting smile faded once the door closed behind them. Interesting how Charlotte could read Marvin's mind, too.

At five, Betsy hurried Godwin through the closing-up process, wrote up a deposit slip for the day's slim profits, and went upstairs to finish packing for the trip to New London.

She was debating whether to pack a light nightie or her pajamas when her doorbell rang. Thinking it was probably Jill, she went to buzz her in and left the door to her apartment ajar while she went back to her packing.

"Hello?" asked a strange voice. Male. She picked up the cell phone she'd been about to put in the big purse she was taking on this trip, and went to peer out the door.

Two men were standing at the end of the little hallway to her living room. They were looking awkward, half prepared to retreat.

"Hello," said Betsy.

"Are you Ms Devonshire?" asked the taller of the pair. He was also the more robust, and likely older, his dark hair thinning and gray at the temples. He was wearing a short-sleeved tan shirt, brown trousers, and dressy shoes.

"Yes. Who are you?"

The shorter one offered a shy smile. He was wearing gold-rimmed glasses, a faded blue shirt, old blue jeans, and thick black sandals. "I'm David Birmingham, and this is my brother Tom. Our sister Lisa seems to think you might want to talk to us."

"I'd love to talk with you, but I don't have much time. I'm leaving for New London."

"Oh, are you involved with the run this weekend?" asked Tom.

"Yes, I'm a volunteer and I'm sponsoring the Stanley Steamer that Lars Larson is driving."

"Love those Steamers," said Tom with a smile, and Betsy recalled that he owned a car dealership.

"Why is that? Do you sell antique cars?" asked Betsy. "Come in, sit down. May I get you a soft drink?"

"Not for me, thanks," said David.

"Not me, either," said Tom. They came and sat side by side on the loveseat, which was just barely long enough to contain them. He continued, "I sell new and used cars, but not *that* used. The Steamer was a remarkable car for its time, and many people are fascinated at the notion of a steam-powered car. But they never had a chance against the internal combustion engine."

"Why was that?" asked Betsy, taking the upholstered chair at right angles to the loveseat. "Because it had to stop to take on water so often? I understand the later models had condensers."

Tom nodded. "That's right. But steam was inefficient, because it adds a step between the fuel and the wheels. The fuel heats the water to produce steam, which drives the motor, which turns the wheels. An internal combustion engine uses the fuel to drive the motor which turns the wheels. You lose energy every step you take away from the fuel. Those Stanleys got terrible mileage per gallon. On the other hand, I *love* that whistle." He smiled. There was something both slick and charming about him, which, Betsy considered, figured.

"So you've seen Lars's Stanley?"

He shook his head. "No, but one generally turns up at the run, and I've been to a lot of runs."

"Are you going this year?" asked Betsy.

"No." He suddenly looked sad. "Probably won't go again, now that Dad's not gonna be there."

David said, "Lisa said you're investigating our father's death?"

"Yes, informally. I'm not a police investigator or even a private eye. I'm involved because your mother and I spent most of the day together."

The phone in Betsy's hand rang, startling her. She punched the Talk button, said "Excuse me" to the brothers and "Hello?" into the phone.

"Betsy, it's Jill. Are you on the road?"

"No, I'm still at home."

"Oh, well, I was starting to worry about you. I called the motel in Willmar, and you weren't there yet."

Betsy didn't know whether to be grateful for Jill's concern or annoyed at it. "I'll be leaving soon. The two younger Birmingham brothers are here. Tom and David."

"I hope you have something to ask them. And listen to this: We got a report from the medical examiner on time of death and guess what? Time of death could be as long ago as Friday afternoon."

"But we know it can't be that long ago. I saw the man Saturday around eleven."

"Yes, I know. Lars says it's because the body was burned. The ME does say he might have died as late as

Saturday morning. But it wasn't well into Saturday afternoon."

Betsy said, "That still fits, doesn't it? He only went as far as Minnetonka, and that was before noon. Listen, I've got to take care of my company. I'll see you tomorrow, okay?" Betsy hung up.

David said, a little too brightly, "Funny how the phone knows to ring when you have company, isn't it?"

"Yes. Why did you two come to see me?"

Tom said, "We told you, Lisa said you wanted to talk to us."

"I never told her that."

Tom said, "You didn't? Funny, because she said—"

David interrupted, gently but firmly, "All right. Bro said he told you not to poke into this mess we're in, and we decided to talk to you ourselves, to ask you to continue. Independently, actually. Tom called me to see if I knew where you lived. I didn't, but I'd found out you own this building. We came over to see if one of your tenants had your address and we saw your name on one of the mailboxes."

Tom said, "So we rang the doorbell and here we are," putting a chipper face on it.

David said, "Mother told Lisa you investigate crimes. Are you a licensed private investigator as well as a businesswoman? We're prepared to pay you a fee."

"I'm not licensed," Betsy said. "I do this nonprofessionally, strictly as an amateur. I'm actually out to protect the innocent, rather than find evidence of who committed a crime. Of course, that often means finding out who really did it."

"Then this should be right up your alley," said Tom. "Our mother didn't kill our father—you know that, but the way the cops are sniffing around, it looks like they'll try to find a way to charge her."

"I don't see how that could possibly happen," said Betsy. Then a light went on inside her head. "Oh, this isn't about her, is it? It's about Marvin."

Tom said, "How could it be about Marvin?"

But David said, a little too eagerly, "What have you found out?"

"Your sister is wrong, isn't she? This isn't a one-way love affair, Marvin worshiping your mother from afar. Your mother is as much in love with Marvin as he is with her—and you know it."

Tom said, "Maybe. But they never did anything. There wasn't an affair or something."

But David, leaning back out of his brother's line of sight, grimaced at Betsy in disagreement.

Tom went on, "We think Sergeant Steffans suspects Marv and our mother were, er, having an affair." He hesitated, trying to decide if he should deny it again.

David leaped into the breach. "So, you see, that gives Marv a motive, big-time. Mother would never cheat on Father, but she would never leave him for his best friend, either. So Steffans thinks maybe Marv got impatient."

Betsy asked, "What do you think?"

"He's wrong."

Tom said, "I agree. Not Marv Pierce. Not in a million years."

Betsy said, "Is Marvin as wealthy as Bill was?"

Tom said, "What's that got to do with it?"

"Older women may love as ardently as the young, but they've generally developed a pragmatic streak and are less likely to surrender financial security in the name of love."

David nodded. "Otherwise, Mother would have divorced Father years ago."

Tom said indignantly, "She would not!"

David said, "But Mother isn't as rich as she would have been if Father had died before Bro came home."

"I don't understand," said Betsy.

"Father had to give half the company to Bro in order to get him to agree to take over. His will left quote half his property unquote to Mother, and wills mean what they say, not what the testator meant, so that means she gets a quarter of the company instead of half. Most of her and Father's income was the profit from Birmingham Metal, so she's going to have to cut back on her spending big-time."

Betsy said, "Does Sergeant Steffans know this?"

Tom nodded. "He was asking me questions about it. I told him the profits would be less even if Father hadn't died, because Bro is putting the profits into an expansion program. He thinks he can double the company's business."

Betsy said, "Charlotte told me Bill was countermanding some of your brother's orders. I take it there was a power struggle going on."

David said, "Yes. Father liked the company where it was. Very stable, profits very reliable."

Betsy said, "I hope you see that puts Bro very high on the list of suspects."

Tom stared at her. "No. This was another reason to suspect Mother—but she's got an airtight alibi, thanks to you."

David said, "Tommy, maybe you don't know how

mad Bro was about Father not letting go of the company like he promised."

Tommy waved that notion away. "Bro? Not a chance. Bro's too square to murder anyone, much less Father. He's a bigger square than you are."

That set off a mild argument about the merits of being square that Betsy finally interrupted with an announcement that she wanted to be in New London at a reasonable hour. They apologized and left.

Betsy went back to her packing, and as she put her pajamas into the suitcase, she remembered Broward's sincere anger in warning her off—and Lisa's assessment that Bro was a chip off a very aggressive block. Tom and David were wrong. Bro was near if not at the top of Betsy's list of suspects.

Looking around to make sure she'd left nothing behind, Betsy saw her unread copy of the *Excelsior Bay Times* weekly newspaper. Remembering the reporter and photographer at last Saturday's event, she picked it up and put it in her stitchery project bag. Maybe there was a picture of Lars with his Steamer in there.

13

Despite the delay in getting out of town, Betsy took Highway 55 west rather than 12. Twelve was almost a direct line to Willmar, but she wanted a look at both Buffalo and New London, which lay on the other two sides of a triangle formed by the Twin Cities, Willmar, and Paynesville.

Still, she was surprised at how long a drive it was. She knew, on the one hand, that the route the antique cars would drive from New London to the Cities suburb of New Brighton was a trifle over a hundred miles—but the route wandered and meandered to avoid main highways and their traffic. On the other hand, apparently there was only so much meandering a route could do.

The early-evening air was cool, and she rolled down all the windows. Out past Rockford, some farmer had been cutting hay and the sweet scent was paradise. The sun was below the horizon but the sky was still blue when the speed limit dropped and signs announced Buffalo, where the antique cars would pause for lunch on Saturday. Betsy noted the turnoff for the high school was on the eastern side of the town, and marked by a gas station. She'd be coming here to help prepare and serve lunch on Saturday. The highway skirted Buffalo's downtown, so she couldn't tell if it was a brisk little city on the move, or a dying country town full of sad, boarded-up commercial buildings.

At Paynesville she turned south on Highway 23, which went past New London on its way to Willmar. By the time she got there, it had been completely dark for a long while, and she didn't get even a vague impression of what New London was like.

By then she was tired, and Willmar was twenty long minutes away. She turned on the radio and found a talk show with a very aggravating host. Being annoyed got her adrenaline flowing, and she came into Willmar bright with anger.

In Minnesota it's hard to find a city, town, or village that isn't wrapped around, alongside, or divided by a lake. Willmar was no exception. Highway 23 joined a divided highway as it ran along the water. A frontage road appeared on the other side of the highway, and soon after Betsy saw the sign for her motel. She pulled into the graveled parking area with a sigh of relief, signed in, called Jill to report her safe arrival, and went to bed.

But she was still too annoyed to sleep. She got into her project bag and found she'd left her knitting in Excelsior—another annoyance. She'd been working on an infant's sweater for a homeless program, and forgot she'd brought it down to the shop to show a customer. The counted pattern she had brought along was too complex to tackle for relaxation, so she picked up the *Bay Times*. There was no story about the antique cars on the front page, or the second page, or the fourth page—there it was, a two-page spread in the very center, with lots of photographs. One was of Lars, standing in streamers of steam like a character in a Gothic movie, his expression serious and his pose dramatic. Jill might like a print of that. Betsy made a note in the margin to call the paper and ask if prints were for sale. There were more than a dozen photos surrounding a short article in the middle of the spread. In an upper corner was the 1902 Oldsmobile, and there was the Winton, its cloche-hatted rider standing with one foot on the running board, needing only a machine gun to look a lot like Clyde's girlfriend, Bonnie. In a lower corner was a white-flannel rump sticking out from under the hood of a Maxwell. "Getting to the seat of the problem," read the caption, "an unidentified driver works on his Maxwell." Bill Birmingham had said he didn't want to be interviewed, Betsy remembered, and apparently hadn't paused in his labors even long enough to give his name. Cute photo, in a way, and an even cuter caption—but too bad the last photograph of Bill had to be this ridiculous pose. Such a contrast to the noble look the photographer had somehow found in Lars.

Betsy yawned. Amusement had washed away her annoyance, and suddenly she was very tired. She folded the paper and put it on the nightstand, turned out the light, and in less than five minutes was sound asleep in her rented bed.

A loud noise startled her out of a dreamless sleep. For a moment she couldn't think what the noise was or why the bed felt unfamiliar. Oh, Willmar, sure. And it was the phone, which made its harsh noise again, and she fumbled the receiver to her ear.

"H'lo?" she mumbled.

"Aren't you up yet?" asked a chipper voice she recognized as Jill's. "I was going to buy you breakfast if you were about ready to go."

Up? Was it morning already? Yes, that seemed to be sunshine shining around the edges of the heavy curtain pulled across the window. Wow.

"Are you here in Willmar?" asked Betsy, blinking to get her vision going. She'd had laser surgery on her eyes a few months ago and was still pleased and a little surprised, once she pried them open, to be able to read the little bedside alarm clock without help. Six A.M. Wow.

"No, I'm in New London. There's a nice little café on the main street that knows how to fry an egg just like you want it."

"Poached," said Betsy. "Can they fry it poached?"

"I wouldn't be surprised. In forty-five minutes then?"

"What's the name of the place?"

"I can't remember, but it's the café on the main street, you can't miss it," said Jill. "Lars and I will meet you there."

Must be a really small town, thought Betsy, hanging up and tossing back the covers.

Soon after, she drove into New London across a beautiful curving bridge over a big old millpond. It dropped her off in downtown, which was two blocks long and did not in any way resemble its namesake.

There was a needlework shop, Betsy noticed as she got out of her car, and a gift shop, a restaurant, a gas station, and a café. The café was full of people, and the air was heavy with the old-fashioned, pre-cholesterol-scare smells of bacon, sausage, fried eggs, toast, hash browns, pancakes, and hot, maple-flavored syrup. There was a counter, whose seven stools were made of red plastic and stainless steel, and pale, Formica-topped tables along the other walls. Pictures of wildlife adorned the smokey blue walls.

At a table along the wall were Jill, Lars, and Adam. Lars and Adam were facing the door, and so raised their hands when Betsy came in to show her where they were.

Betsy sat beside Jill, who handed her a menu. "They can poach you an egg if you like," she said. "I already asked."

Lars and Adam were digging into platters laden with Canadian bacon, fried eggs, and hash browns, with toast on the side.

Betsy ordered a poached egg on a slice of whole wheat toast, and coffee. Jill had a gigantic sweet roll with pecans glued to it with melted brown sugar.

Adam smiled at Betsy. "Ready to go for a ride?"

"What, you mean with Lars?"

"Okay, if you like. But there are other cars making the short trip to Litchfield today. You can hitch a ride with one of them, if you like, maybe on the way out or back."

"Gosh, thanks!" said Betsy, glancing at Lars to see if he minded.

He shrugged and smiled around a mouthful of potato.

"Do I have some duties to perform today?" Betsy asked Adam.

"Not really. We're not logging people out for Litchfield, it's an informal trip."

"Are you driving to Litchfield?" she asked.

"Yes. You want to ride with me? I'm driving my 1911 Renault sport touring car. You won't see another like it in your life."

Betsy asked, "Do you mean because it's restored so beautifully, or because it's rare?"

Adam grinned. "Both."

"Well, how can I turn down a double once-in-a-lifetime opportunity? Though I probably won't appreciate it like I should. I'm so ignorant about this car-collecting business."

Adam's grin broadened. "Just watch the envious eyes on us, and you'll know all you need to know."

Lars said, "You want to make the return trip with Jill and me?"

Betsy looked at Jill. "You're finally coming to terms with that car, aren't you?"

"I suppose so. I went for a ride in it a few days ago, and I have to admit, it's slick."

"Next year, in costume!" announced Betsy happily. To Lars she said, "Yes, I'll be glad to ride with you."

Jill asked Adam, "Is there a layover in Litchfield, or do we just go there and come right back?"

"Whatever you like. Since we don't note departure times for these little practice runs, you're entirely on your own. But if you're interested in staying awhile, Litchfield has a nice Civil War museum, and some antique shops."

Betsy wondered what sort of Civil War museum

there could be in a place so far removed from the battle sites—and decided she'd take a look and see. She looked at Jill and thought she detected the same notion.

Lars did, too. He sighed. "All right, we'll take a look at the museum."

Betsy smiled at yet another instance of someone knowing someone else's mind very well. "What time are you leaving, Adam?" she asked.

"About ten, if things are running all right at the Boy Scout building. That's our headquarters here in New London." He checked his watch. "I'd better get over there. See you at ten." He smiled at Jill and Lars. "You, too," he said, rose, and departed.

As soon as he was out of earshot, Lars said, "So what have you found out so far?"

"About what?" asked Betsy.

"About this murder," he said impatiently.

"Nothing."

His light blue eyes widened. "I don't believe that," he said.

"Why not?"

"You're too clever to have gone around asking questions like you do and not found out *something*."

Jill said, mock-proudly, "And you thought he was just another dumb blond, didn't you?"

Lars guffawed, but his eyes remained expectantly on Betsy.

"All right. I have been told by two of her children that a friend of the Birmingham family was hopelessly in love with Charlotte. I think she returned that love, and may have been having a long-term affair with him. His name is Marvin Pierce, and I have a sad feeling that since Charlotte wouldn't divorce her husband for him, he may have found another way to set her free."

"If they were mutually in love, why wouldn't Charlotte divorce her husband?" asked Jill. "From what I've heard, Bill Birmingham was a workaholic, and when he did come home, he was a tyrant. Why not leave him? Divorce is easy enough nowadays."

Lars said, "Maybe she was afraid of Bill's reaction. If he was bad-tempered, was he also abusive?"

"I don't know," said Betsy. "I haven't heard anything on that order."

"Well, what else do you know?" asked Lars.

Betsy said, "Bill Birmingham was a very wealthy man, wealthier than Marvin. If it wasn't me supplying the alibi, I'd certainly be trying to poke a hole in it, because Charlotte is the obvious suspect. On the other hand, Bill's death came at a bad time. It seems a substantial part of his income was the profits from his company. When Bill had a ministroke, he invited his son Broward to come home and take over the business. Bro has all kinds of ideas for expanding the company, and he'd been plowing the profits back into it. Bill was trying to stop him, but not only had Bill turned the management over to Bro, he had to give half the company to Bro to get him to agree to come home. Bill was taking steps to stop or at least slow Bro down when he was killed."

"Where does that leave the grieving widow?" asked Lars.

"Not as well off as she'd have been if she'd killed Bill before Bro came into the picture."

"Ah," nodded Jill.

Lars asked, "Where was Bro Saturday morning?"

"I don't know. Is there a way to find out, maybe from

Sergeant Steffans? I don't want to ask Bro myself—he has his father and grandfather's bad temper."

Jill pulled a notebook from her shirt pocket—Betsy was amused to notice that even out of uniform Jill carried one—and made a note. Writing, she said, "I wonder if Marvin is as eager a lover now that Charlotte's not rich?"

"Well, I'm not sure how not-rich she is. I'd like to find out the situation with Bill's estate. Surely there's more to it than the business and a set of antique cars."

Jill made another note. "Looks like I'll have to take Sergeant Steffans to lunch next week." She was so busy writing she missed the massive frown that slowly formed on Lars's broad forehead.

Sergeant Steffans ran his thumb and long, knobby fingers down either side of his narrow jaw. He was standing in Marvin's small office in the Lutheran Brotherhood Building downtown. Lutheran Brotherhood was a large insurance company with headquarters in a blood-red building with copper-coated windows, one of a set of buildings apparently colored by a comic-book artist on the south end of downtown Minneapolis. Steffans grew up in St. Paul, whose sedate old skyscrapers and narrow streets show plainly why it considers itself at best a fraternal twin to Minneapolis's broad avenues and sci-fi buildings.

Marvin Pierce was about five-nine, with light brown hair in a very retro crew cut. He was trim and athletic in build, dressed Friday casual in Dockers, sport coat, and blue dress shirt without a tie. His face couldn't carry the build or the hair, being very ordinary and middle-aged. His blue eyes were wary.

"It's just routine," Steffans said. "We have to check and double-check every possibility." He could see Marvin didn't believe that, but it was true—most cases were broken by following a well-marked routine.

"I didn't see her Saturday morning," Marvin said, "so I don't know what time she left her house. I know she was home by five-thirty, because that's what time it was when I checked my watch when I was in her kitchen heating water to make her a cup of tea. I'd been there about, oh, I'm not sure, twenty minutes? But of course, by then, Bill'd been dead for hours." He bit his lip and stroked the top of his head, yanking his hand away when he encountered the bristly haircut. New style then. Was that important? Steffans wrote a very brief note— he was a thorough note taker—while Marvin mused, "God, what a mess! I still can't believe he's gone."

"How long had you known him?"

"Years." When Steffans held his pen ready and looked inquiring, Marvin calculated and said, "Twenty-six, twenty-seven years. Maybe twenty-eight. I worked for him for a while, foreman in the plant."

"Why'd you quit?"

"Got a better offer, which wasn't difficult. Bill Birmingham hated to pay a man what he was worth. Not a bad boss, a little hard, and tight. Good businessman and better friend. Liked him, liked his kids, liked his wife."

"You married?"

"Twice, once right out of high school, lasted ten months, no kids; then nine years to Alice. Three kids, all girls, all doing fine, turned out nice. 'Course, a lot of that is due to Alice's second husband, a good man, walked the second two down the aisle when they got married." Marvin was looking inward, a half-smile on his lips, and half of that was pained.

Steffans made another note. "Did you murder Bill Birmingham?"

That directness surprised Marvin; he looked up, mouth half-open, eyes wide. "No," he said.

"Do you know who did?"

"No!" This came out a bit sharply, and he grimaced. "No way I could know that," he said. "I wasn't there when it happened."

"Where were you?"

"At home."

"Alone?"

Now he was amused. "Yes, as it happens. I had some friends over the night before and we sat up late, playing poker, shooting the bull, drinking beer. I got up Saturday, but I was feeling so bad I had to call Buddy Anderson, who I was supposed to meet for golf, and beg off. I don't know if it was the beer or the sandwiches, but I was pretty sick all day Saturday. I stayed home with the TV, so I was there when Char's son Bro called me late in the afternoon with the news, and asked me to come over. Char was taking it hard, he said, and asking for me."

"Were you surprised?"

"Hell, yes! I thought that when old Bill went, it would be a stroke, him having high blood pressure and all."

"No, I mean that Charlotte Birmingham would ask for you."

"Oh. No, not at all. I've sat up with her and one or another of the children many a time. Been there for the good times, too. Done it so much people are surprised to learn I'm not a member of the family."

As she drove behind Jill and Lars around the millpond, Betsy noted small houses of the post–World War II variety, then a wide, grassy field full of motor homes, closed trailers, and antique cars. Jill turned there, and a little farther along were some enormous, modern sheds on one side of the narrow street and on the other an old cemetery. At least some of the enormous sheds were bus barns, their big open doors showing that inside were not city buses, but the luxury kind that are rented to groups making jaunts. Except one of the barns had antique cars inside and in front of it.

There were more antique cars parked on a sandy verge along the narrow lane.

Betsy was so busy looking around that she almost failed to notice that Jill, on making another turn, had immediately pulled onto that scrubby verge. She slammed on her brakes as she went past Jill's car, and pulled in at the far end of the row, beside a sky-blue vehicle the size of a Conestoga wagon. It had blue and white striped awning material for a roof. The hood was small for a car that size, and the radiator sloped backward from its base. Like most of the antique cars, its wheels were wagon size, with thick, wooden spokes. When she got out, she could hear that the car's engine was running, but in a very peculiar manner. Every antique car she had met so far had its own motor sound, but this one had to be the strangest. *Brum*-sniff, *brum*-sniff, *brum*-sniff, it went.

Jill and Lars were walking up to an old, white clapboard house. There was a big sign, BOY SCOUTS OF

AMERICA, over a screen door marked only by a small concrete slab. Betsy took two steps to follow, then turned to listen some more to the huge car's motor. Yes, it was inhaling sharply between short engine sounds, *brum*-sniff, *brum*-sniff, *brum*-sniff. A man in jeans and blue checked shirt who had ducked around Lars on the walk now came angling toward Betsy.

"Whaddaya think?" he asked as he stopped beside her.

"What is it?" asked Betsy.

"A 1901 Winton. Single cylinder. This is the car that made a transcontinental crossing of the United States, New York to San Francisco, before there were paved roads or gas stations."

"Wow," said Betsy. "The pioneering spirit was still alive then, I guess."

That remark pleased him. "And I own a hunk of it." The man got in and put his machine into reverse. Whining and tilting dangerously, it backed onto the lane, but then rolled smoothly on down toward the bus barns. Apparently it only sniffed while idling.

Must be a heck of a big cylinder, thought Betsy, *if you can hear it sucking wind like that. Of course, to move something that big, it would have to be one heck of a cylinder.*

She went up the walk and through the screen door— which made a very nostalgic creak when opened and a satisfactory slap when it closed. But this wasn't a home. The floor was faded linoleum tile; the walls were dotted with Boy Scout posters and an old black bearskin.

They had come in through the long side of a rectangular room. Tables of assorted sizes and styles were scattered around it. Behind a long one made of plywood, under the bearskin, stood three women and two household-moving-size cardboard boxes. On a nearby table was a stack of the banners drivers were to put on their cars, canvas squares with ANTIQUE CAR RUN, the soft drink symbol, and big black numbers printed on them. Ties ran off each corner.

The women behind the table were all wearing big green T-shirts with the logo of the Antique Car Run printed on their fronts. Half a dozen men and four women waited patiently in two lines in front of the table. Lars and Jill were among them.

One man at the head of the line was laughing at some jest he'd already made, and as the woman handed him a shirt and a clear plastic bag of materials, he asked, "What's the difference between roast beef and pea soup?"

"What?" asked the woman.

"Anyone can roast beef!" he said. She made a "get away with you" gesture at him, and he turned to leave, laughing heartily. *I bet he started out as a traveling salesman,* thought Betsy.

On the long table was a big computer printout listing each driver's name, hometown, kind of car, and number of passengers. When it was his turn, Lars announced, "I'm Lars Larson, number sixty-three," and one of the women ran a finger down the list. When she found it, she ran a highlighter mark through it.

"Welcome to New London, Lars," she said. "Are these your two riders?" she added, smiling at Betsy and Jill.

Jill nodded, and Betsy said, "No, but I'm a volunteer. I'll be logging departures tomorrow."

Another woman, very brisk and tiny, asked Lars, "What size T-shirt do you wear, dear?"

"Two-X," he replied, and she asked the same question of Jill and Betsy, then turned to one of the enormous boxes, which came up to her armpits, to dig around until she found examples in the right sizes.

"We've got to get these sorted out," she remarked to the woman with the marker. "Or I'll fall in reaching for one and never be seen again. Here you go, dears." Then she turned to lift out a clear plastic bag from the other box. It held maps and instructions.

The other woman said to Lars, "Tie your banner on the left side of your car. That's where the monitors will be standing, and they'll want to be able to find your number quickly if you come in with several other cars."

Lars grinned. "I won't be among several other cars, I'll be way out in front."

The woman frowned severely at him. "Remember, this is *not* a race."

Jill snorted faintly and Betsy smiled. Not officially, no. But the cars were mostly being driven by men used to overcoming competition, and who did not like losing.

14

As they went down the walk out of the Boy Scout building, Betsy checked her watch. It was not quite quarter to ten, so she continued across the narrow lane and through an opening in a tall hedge into the cemetery.

"What's up?" asked Jill, hurrying to join her.

"Nothing, we have a few minutes, so I thought I'd look around."

"In here?" asked Lars. "This is a cemetery," he added, in case she hadn't noticed the headstones.

"I know. I just like cemeteries." Betsy said it somewhat shamefacedly.

"So do I," said Jill.

"You do?"

"I thought you'd got over that!" groaned Lars. "I don't get it, what's the attraction?"

Betsy said, "I like the epitaphs. They're coming back, you know. For a long while it was too costly to put more than names and a date on a tombstone, but with laser cutters, you can have drawings and sayings all over your stone. Every so often I try to think up one for myself. I like really old ones best. 'Behold O man, as you pass by—' "

Jill joined in, " 'As you are now, so once was I. As I am now, you soon must be. Repent, prepare to follow me.' " Jill and Betsy laughed quietly, pleased to find another thing in common.

Lars said, "I'm going to go start my car," and walked away.

"He's a little sensitive," apologized Jill. "Or are we a little mad?"

"There's something peaceful about cemeteries," said Betsy. "I think long, easy thoughts in these places. Oh, look at that stone with the bus on it!"

"Someone in the Boy Scout building said the man who owned the bus company was buried here so he could keep watch over his company."

A large monument near where they came in had lettering on every side. They paused to read it and found an account of an Indian massacre, noting the remains of the victims were buried here. "Say, you don't see many of these," said Jill.

"I know. From the cowboy movies you'd think they'd be common, but they're not."

They heard a quiet voice, and moved sideways just enough to see a woman on the other side, talking to a man taking photographs of the monument. She was saying—not reading from the monument, which had the usual sentiments about savages and innocent settlers,

". . . and the local Indian agent told them that the money promised from the federal government in payment for their land was not coming and they could try surviving that winter by eating grass. So of course, they got upset."

"Uh-huh," said the man. "Here, come point at the writing so I can show in the picture how big this sucker is."

"Come on," murmured Jill, and Betsy followed her back through the hedge.

They went the short distance down the lane and then crossed the faded blacktop street to the bus barn. Drivers, some wearing the big white dusters of the period, were standing beside their machines, or tinkering with them, or running a chamois or soft cloth over them, or talking with others about adventures on the road.

It was indicative of the determined goodwill these people had for one another that they said nothing when Lars began the lengthy process of firing up his Stanley. Steamers make internal combustion people nervous. Lars did his part by rolling his machine out of the shed first. Betsy came to help push and was surprised to find the car light and easy to move. "No transmission to weigh things down," Lars reminded her.

While Lars worked with his blow torch, Betsy went to look at the other cars preparing for departure. Some she had seen in Excelsior last Saturday.

Trembling like Don Knotts was the rickety, topless, curved-dash Oldsmobile. Near it was an ancient green Sears, whose tiller came up from the side and made a ninety-degree turn to lay across the driver's lap. The International Harvester farm wagon with hard rubber tires came rolling by.

Here also was the immense Winton's younger sibling, the soft-yellow car with brown fenders that could have passed as a car from the twenties, that had beat Lars to Excelsior. And there was another, brighter yellow car of very dashing design. It had wide tires, a very long hood, two seats, and a big oval gas tank on top of the trunk, right behind the seats. On the back bumper was a spare tire with a black canvas cover on which was printed MARMON, 1911. Like the Winton, it looked very competent, and she began to feel a little better about being here with the super-capable Stanley.

Falling somewhere in between the Olds and the Marmon were a black 1910 Maxwell two-seater and an immense dark blue Cadillac touring car from 1911. There was also a beautiful, snub-nosed two-seater Buick, bright red, with its name spelled in brass on its radiator and *1907* in smaller figures.

An early REO pickup truck, also red, with hard rubber wheels, *buck-whuddled* by, an enormous American flag flying from the bin. "John!" called someone as he went by, "you're not allowed to use a sail!"

John, laughing, answered, "That's *my* line, Vern!"

A little yellow Brush with its top up puttered along behind the REO, driven by a man who looked a great deal like Oliver Hardy. Behind it *dick-dicked* a red Yale whose driver and passenger were wearing white knickers and jackets, pinch-brim hats, and goggles. The car, Betsy noticed, had a back door one could use to get into the back seat. "What year?" she called to the driver.

"Ought five!" he replied and waved as he continued up the road.

There came an eerie sound, a low howling slowly climbing the scale as it grew louder. Heads turned in alarm toward it, then just as Betsy recognized it as the Stanley building a head of steam, someone said, "By God, you'll never get me up in one of those things!" and there was laughter.

"Hey, Betsy!" called Lars. "Com'ere!" She waved and went over.

Jill said, "We're going to leave now. Have you met up with Adam?"

"No." Betsy looked around, but didn't see him. "You go ahead, I'll find him."

Jill followed Lars into the car, the route papers in her hand. "We go south, which is the way we're headed," she said, looking at the directions. She waved at Betsy. "See you in Litchfield!"

Lars politely waited until he was well away from the bus barn before blowing his whistle, but still some people waved impolitely at him.

When all but one of the cars going on the jaunt had departed, Betsy was still standing there. The driver of that last car, a tall, slim man with nice blue eyes said, "Miss your ride?"

"I don't see how," Betsy replied. "I was supposed to go with Adam Smith in his Renault."

"Last I saw him, he was in the Boy Scout building," said the man, climbing down. "That was just a few minutes ago, but he looked all tied up."

Betsy's face fell and he said, "Why don't you ride with us? Plenty of room." He gestured at his car, a big Model T. A woman sitting in the passenger seat waved invitingly.

Betsy hesitated. She wanted to talk to Adam. On the other hand, if he was really tied up, she was not only not going to talk to him in any case, she wasn't going to get to ride in one of these pioneers. "All right. I have a ride back, which I won't get if I can't get to Litchfield. I'm Betsy Devonshire."

"Mike Jimson. That's my wife Dorothy. Climb aboard. Spark retarded?" he asked his wife.

"Yes, love," she said.

Betsy opened the door and climbed into the spacious back seat, which was black leather and deeply comfortable. Mike cranked once, then again, and the Model T shook itself to life. He came around and got in, as his wife said, "South on Oak to the Stop sign at County Road Forty."

Used to the incredible smoothness of the Stanley, and the very faint vibration of her own modern car, she was a little surprised at the steady jiggle of the Model T, and suddenly empathetic of Charlotte's complaint last weekend of an upset stomach.

There was a line of six antiques waiting to cross Highway 23. The old cars were slow getting into motion, and so needed the road to be clear a considerable distance in both directions. Looking up the line, Betsy was amused to see how it was sort of like looking at a movie slightly out of focus, as each car vibrated to its own rhythm.

When the Model T's turn came, they waited only a couple of minutes before Mike raced his engine, and, the gearbox groaning loudly, they went slowly, slowly up the slight incline and out onto the highway. They were only up to walking speed as they started down the other side, and a modern car whizzing by on the highway tooted its horn derisively.

But now there was a clear stretch, and Mike, relaxing,

suddenly burst into song. Dorothy immediately joined in:

"Let me call you Lizzie, I'm in love with you;
Let me hear you rattle down the av-e-nue;
Keep your headlights glowing, and your taillight, too;
Let me call you Lizzie, I'm in debt for you!"

Betsy laughed. "Who wrote that?" she asked.

"Who knows?" Dorothy replied. "It was a schoolyard song when I was young, though it might have been a vaudeville number about the time the first Model T came out. The Model T was called Tin Lizzie, you know."

"Yes, that's one thing I knew about them. So I guess that song is as old as the joke that you could have a Model T in any color you wanted, so long as it was black."

"Do you know why all Fords were black?" asked Mike.

"Why?" asked Betsy, expecting another joke.

But Mike was serious. "Two reasons: first, because black paint dried quicker than any other color; and second, because it made supplying spare parts a snap. No need to try to figure out how many green fenders or blue doors or brown hood covers to stock when everything came in black. And all the parts were interchangeable, thanks to the assembly line method. People forget what a huge innovator Henry Ford was. He once said he could give his Model T's away and make money just selling parts."

When they got onto County Road 2, which was a busy two-lane highway, the old cars had to run on the shoulder. Cars rushed past, some honking in greeting, others in warning, one or two in anger. Mike summoned the Ford's best speed, which came with even more noise and so much vibration Betsy wondered why parts weren't shaken free.

"How fast are we going?" she asked, her voice sounding flat against the racket.

Mike checked his primitive instrument panel. "Twenty-eight mind-blowing miles an hour. What's next?" he asked Dorothy.

"We're on this for six miles," she replied, "until we come to a Stop sign where Route Ten joins us and we turn left."

"Okay," he nodded.

Betsy tried to relax in the capacious back seat, stretching her arms out on either side. *Seize the day,* she told herself. The breeze made her light dress flutter against her legs, and kept her cool. She had wisely dabbed sun block on her face and arms this morning, so no fear of sunburn. She decided she liked riding up high and having her feet flat on the floor instead of resting on their heels. And in the open like this, and at this slow a speed, there was plenty of time to look around and enjoy the sights and smells of the country-side. Unlike in the Stanley, with its low sides, in the Model T she felt very much "inside" and safe, and so didn't mind the lack of a seat belt very much.

But the noise was such that she soon gave up trying to talk with Mike and Dorothy.

In a little over an hour they came into Pine Grove and pulled over behind a row of antique cars for a pit stop at the Home Town Café. Betsy climbed out, dusty, windblown, and a little deaf from the noise of the en-

gine. She crossed the highway, surprised at her un-
steady pace. That jiggle was really something,
especially when it stopped.

Pine Grove was a hamlet strung along one side of
the highway, the other side marked by a well-
maintained railroad line. She looked around, at the
dusty buildings, the flat landscape, the old cars. She'd
admired the people who made the movie *Paper Moon*
for traveling around the Midwest in a search for authentic dirt roads and small towns, thinking then it must
have been hard to find them; but they'd traveled down
a dirt road a while back, and here was an authentically
shabby little town, right on a highway, not hard to find
at all.

Betsy felt as if her brain had shaken loose during the
ride. She had gone into some strange, reflective mode—
not the kind that comes from actual meditation, but the
kind that comes from heavy-duty pain pills. Everything
had become a tinge unreal. She saw an elderly man
sitting very erect on a bench in front of the café, and
wanted to go ask him if he'd fought in the Civil War,
just to see if he'd cackle and tell her a story about
Gettysburg. Of course, another part of her knew that
question was better asked of the old man's great-
grandfather, that she was caught up in the pseudo-
reality of a moving picture. This was the early
twenty-first century, not the early twentieth. Right? She
began to look for an anachronism to prove it. Like in
the movie *Gladiator*, spoiled for her when the ancient
Romans handed out hastily printed leaflets. The movie
makers had apparently forgotten the printing press was
at least ten centuries forward from ancient Rome.

And now, here came a good anachronism in the form

of a train rumbling down the tracks behind the row of cars. The engines pulling the train were diesels, which didn't replace steam engines until the fifties. She waved gratefully at it, and watched the whole train rumble by. It was long, mostly grain cars. There was no little red caboose at the end, which made her feel sad.

She went into the café and bought a Diet Coke, which came in an aluminum can. Aluminum, she knew, was once an extremely rare metal, so rare that the builders of the Washington Monument paid huge sums for enough to cap the point, forgoing the far less expensive gold or platinum.

Times change in unexpected ways, she reflected, and no period movie ever gets it exactly right. Especially when it came to women's hairdos; no matter how authentic the costumes, you could always tell when a movie was made by the way the lead actress wore her hair.

The people were sitting at tables talking about cars and the trip, but also about other things: "It's not the size of the boat, but its ability to stay in port until all the passengers have disembarked," said a man in a low voice with a hint of a snigger in it. He was the same man who earlier couldn't "pea" soup.

A woman was saying to another woman, "And then, darling, when the judge called for a trot, that woman behind me went into a *rack,* I am not kidding, a *rack! And* the judge gave her the blue ribbon! I nearly fell off my horse, but decided instead I'd had enough of showing Arabians, and I sold Sheik's Desire the next week and bought the Yale that Tom had been panting after."

A man boasted with a hint of regret, "I had her up

to forty last week, on that downhill slope on County
Five, but she was shaking so hard I thought a wheel
had come loose. She hasn't been the same since. I think
she scared herself. I know she scared me."

Betsy didn't see Lars and Jill, but that didn't surprise
her; she hadn't seen the Stanley outside, either. They
must have already stopped and gone on, or not stopped
at all, more likely. After having been beaten last Saturday, Lars was probably determined to arrive first in
Litchfield.

Although this was not, of course, a race.

What was a bit more problematic was that Mike and
Dorothy weren't there, either.

Betsy took her Coke outside, to be reassured by the
sight of the Model T still parked across the street. *They
must be in the restrooms,* she thought. Two drivers
came out and started cranking their cars. The driver of
the REO had to adjust his magneto twice before the
engine caught. *Grunge, grunge, grunge,* it complained,
before he pulled out well behind the other and *putt, putt,
putt-putt-putt,* started up the road.

She watched him diminish to a heat-waved mirage
then heard a sound—not quite like a modern car, but
not like the rickety sound of an old one, either. She
turned and saw something spectacular coming up the
road, to pull off behind the Model T.

It was a gorgeous antique limousine, tall and long, a
rich, royal blue with inlaid brass stripes on the hood
and along the back door. The back seat was under a
black leather roof, but the front seat wasn't. There was
a kind of second windshield behind the front seat, with
hinged wings to further enclose the rear passenger compartment, which appeared to be empty. The very dis-

tinctive hood sloped downward to the nose, then sloped very steeply down and forward to the front bumper. The radiator was *behind* the hood, sticking out around the edges. The tires were fat, the heavy wooden spokes of the wheels painted creamy white. The engine, ticking gently over, stopped, and a man shifted over to the passenger side and climbed out. He was slim, broad-shouldered, and extremely elegant in royal blue riding pants, the old-fashioned kind with wings, and black leather gaiters with buckles. He wasn't wearing a coat or jacket, but an immaculate white shirt whose upper sleeves were encircled by royal blue garters, and as he got out, he took off a royal blue cap with a narrow black bill and wiped his brow with the back of his hand.

Betsy suddenly recognized him. "Adam!" she called.

He looked over at her and smiled and waved his cap.

Betsy looked both ways and hurried across. "Oh my, oh my, oh my!" she said. "Is *this* the Renault? Golly, what a car! Was it made by the same people who make Renaults today? I've never seen anything so elegant!"

"Yes and yes," said Adam, pleased at her enthusiasm. "And I agree, it's about as elegant as a car can get. Body and chassis by Renault, who of course still make cars, running board boxes by Louis Vuitton, who still make luggage, headlamps by Ducellier and ignition by Bosch, both of whom are still in the automotive business."

"What is that half-a-top called, a landau?"

"No, a Victoria."

Betsy swept her eyes down its length. "Gosh, it must be twenty feet long! I didn't know they made limos this far back!"

He laughed. "It's not really a limo, but a sport touring

car. It's seventeen feet long, seven and a half feet tall with the top up."

"Does it have a speaking tube? You know"—she mimed holding something between thumb and two fingers—"home, James," she said in plummy accents.

"As a matter of fact, it does."

"The engine compartment doesn't look very big—how fast does it go?"

"It has four cylinders, which for 1911, the year it was built, is pretty good. She'll do about fifty on a level stretch, if it's long enough. She's heavy, so it takes a couple of miles to get to her top speed. She has a big muffler, so the ride is both smooth and very quiet."

"Wow, I can't get over it, this is so beautiful! I'm so glad you were able to catch up. Mike Jimson told me you got busy just about the time we were supposed to leave, so I rode with him and his wife in their Model T." Betsy gestured toward the car parked ahead of the Renault.

"I'm glad I caught up before you left Pine Grove. But come on, I need something cold to drink before we head out."

They waited for a truck and two cars to pass, all honking at them, one swerving while the driver and his passengers waved madly. While Adam got his can of root beer, Betsy found Mike and Dorothy at a table in the back and explained that she was going to continue the trip in Adam Smith's Renault.

"So Adam got here after all," said Mike. "Good for him. And you're gonna love riding in that thing."

As they went back across the road, Adam asked, "Front or back?"

"Oh, front, so we can talk."

"Wait till I get her started, then." He went to the front of the car, Betsy following, to push a short lever by its brass knob with his left hand, and began to crank with his right. The engine went *fffut-fffut*, he released the lever, and the car started.

"What is that, some kind of spring windup mechanism?" she asked.

"No, the lever is a compression release. It opens the exhaust valves a little so it's easier to crank. Here—" He pointed to a small silver knob on the front—"this is what retards or advances the spark on the magneto, so the car won't backfire and break your cranking arm." He went to climb in, Betsy following.

She looked across the road and saw a small crowd gathered on the sidewalk, some of them fellow antique car drivers.

"You'd think they'd be used to seeing this," said Betsy.

"No, I don't bring this one out very often. It's really rare and it would be a pity if it got in an accident."

The notion of an accident made her reach for her seat belt, which of course wasn't there. "Do you ever think of having seat belts installed?"

"Nope. I only put back what once was there," he said with a smile.

"Do you want me to navigate?"

"No need. I helped lay out this route, so I know it pretty well."

They rode in silence for a bit. The Renault had the weighty, comfortable feel of a big sixties convertible, but the inside wasn't much like a modern car—especially the blank dashboard.

"How do you know how fast you're going?" Betsy asked.

"Look down on the floor near my feet." Sure enough, the speedometer was on the floor. "And the key to turn on the ignition is on the seat, behind my legs. This car has many unique features. You notice there's plenty of room up here."

"Yes?" said Betsy.

"Makers of chauffeur-driven cars wanted to give as much room as possible to the passengers, so the driver's compartment was very small. That's one reason there was a fad for Asian chauffeurs, who, generally being smaller, weren't as cramped."

"That's the kind of trivia that could win someone a lot of money," said Betsy laughing. "All right, why was the driver of this car given more room?"

"Because this wasn't really a limo, and the buyer needed a driver who could double as a bodyguard, someone big enough to need extra space."

"What was this, a gangster's car?"

Adam laughed. "No, not at all."

Betsy was pleased to have put Adam in a good mood, but a little silence fell while she tried to think how to phrase her next question. At last she simply began, "Adam, what do you think happened to Bill Birmingham?"

"What do you mean, what do I think happened? Someone shot him and set his car on fire."

"Who?"

He frowned at her briefly, then returned his eyes to the road. "How should I know?"

"Well, who would want to do such a thing?"

"I don't want to say," he said. "It's hard to think it

might be someone I know." His attitude was so sincere, Betsy began to worry she was on the wrong track entirely. She thought again how to continue, but before she could say anything, he went on. "His son Bro, obviously."

She said, "Because he wanted the business?"

"Because his father wouldn't quit the business like he was supposed to. That was Bill all over, couldn't let go. He just couldn't let go."

"Is that why he wouldn't sell you the Fuller?"

"What?" He glanced at her, frowning deeply. "What are you getting at?"

"He bought that Fuller because you wanted it, right? His original intention was to sell it to you at a profit. But maybe once he got hold of it, he just couldn't let it go."

Adam considered this. "Maybe. But it's more likely he hung on to it in order to make me as mad at him as he was at me. Stick your arm out."

"What?"

"I want to pass the Sears, stick your arm out."

Betsy glanced at the road behind, saw it was clear, and extended her left arm. Adam pulled smoothly out onto the highway, went around the Sears with a wave, and pulled back onto the shoulder again. The Sears sounded its bulb horn and Adam replied with a beautiful French horn note.

They rode in silence for a bit, then Betsy said, "Bill was mad at you because you bought that Maxwell he wanted, right?"

"Partly. But mostly because I ran against him for president of the Antique Car Club. And I beat him. He would have made a lousy president because he didn't

know the meaning of compromise, and everyone knew
it. He thought he lost because I was spreading ugly
rumors about him."

"What kind of rumors?"

"That he rarely listened to what anyone else said, and
if he did happen to hear a good idea, he'd take it as his
own without giving credit. Which weren't rumors, they
were facts, and I said as much in the course of a free
and open campaign."

This time Betsy held her tongue on purpose, and after
a minute, Adam said, "And because he heard that if he
got elected, Charlie and Mack and I would quit and start
our own club. And that after six months ours would be
the only antique car club in Minnesota."

"Did you say those things, too?"

"Well, yes. But I was only repeating what Mack said
first. Besides, it was God's truth."

"I imagine he was pretty angry with you."

"I imagine he was. The truth can hurt."

"Are you going to buy the Fuller from Charlotte?"

"Yes, if she offers it for sale. And if I'm not in
prison, convicted of murdering Bill."

"You think that's possible?"

"Ms. Devonshire, anything's possible. I've been
reading about those convicts on death row they're finding didn't do it after all, and let me tell you, it's keeping
me up at night."

"Minnesota doesn't have the death penalty."

"If they did, I'd've moved to Costa Rica by now."

Soon they turned onto County 11 and a few miles
later entered Litchfield. It was a small city with a really
wide main street which put Betsy in mind of some New
England towns she'd visited long ago. They'd passed a

few of the slower antique cars along the way, but Lars's Stanley was already parked at the top of the street that bordered a pretty little park. He was making some arcane adjustment to the valves when Betsy came up to him.

"Were you the first to arrive?" she asked.

"Of course," he replied, a little too carelessly.

"Where's Jill?"

"Over in the museum." He nodded his head sideways and Betsy looked over at a modest building with a Civil War era cannon in front of it. "I went in with her, but it's just some old pictures and stuff, so I got bored after a while and decided to check my pilot light. If I leave the pilot light on, it keeps a head of steam on and I can start 'er right up."

Betsy said, "How long before you want to start back?"

"Oh, anytime you two are ready. I proved my point today already, and I'll take her easy on the trip back, so she'll be in good trim for tomorrow." And a big, confident grin spread all over his face.

15

The main room on the first floor of the museum was devoted mostly to enlarged photographs of every Litchfield man who had served in the Civil War. There were about twenty, most of them with names like Svenson and Larson and Pedersen. Brief bios under the oval frames indicated some had been in America only a year or two before marching off to war. Betsy found herself touching the frame around the solemn face of a young man who hadn't been in Minnesota long enough to learn English, but had died at Bull Run, age twenty.

Elsewhere on the ground floor was a small collection of dresses from the 1890s. The pride of the collection was made of light green silk, all ruffles and gathers and ruching, worn by a bride at her wedding. It must have been put away carefully, since it showed few signs of wear or fading. But the dress was on a mannequin from the midtwentieth century, when notions of what made a woman's form beautiful were quite different. The dress wasn't designed for a cantilevered bosom, and the mannequin, despite a look of cool indifference, looked as if she would have preferred a pair of pedal pushers and a sleeveless shirt, maybe with a Peter Pan collar.

Betsy went upstairs and found Jill wandering among a large collection of toys. There were electric trains and windup cars and dolls in great variety. "I used to have a doll just like that," said Betsy, pointing to a doll with a composition head and cloth body. "It makes me feel old to see it in a museum."

"Maybe you are old," said Jill, deadpan.

"Oh, yeah? Look over there," retorted Betsy, pointing at a Barbie doll. "I bet you had one of those."

"You want to know the truth? I didn't. My mother didn't like dolls that looked like miniature grownups, and anyway, I preferred baby dolls or little kid dolls. My favorite doll was Poor Pitiful Pearl—remember her?"

"Gosh, yes! She made me think of Wednesday Addams. Remember the old television show? *Biddle-dee-boop!*" She snapped her fingers twice. *"Biddle-dee-boop!"* Snap, snap.

Jill smiled. "Did you get to ride with Adam Smith?"

"Yes, from Pine Grove to here. Jill, you should see his car, it's a 1911 Renault sport touring car seventeen feet long. Gorgeous, gorgeous car, rides like a limo. It's right out front, he parked behind the Stanley."

"How fast does it go?"

"Around fifty."

"Rats, we'd better get back to Lars." Jill started for the stairs.

"Why?" asked Betsy, hurrying to keep up.

"Because when he finds out how fast that car is, he'll go nuts waiting for us. Let's go!"

Sure enough, Lars was in a fever to be gone. "Smith already left in his blue yacht. That Renault's hot, and he doesn't have to stop for water."

"You got steam?" asked Jill.

"Yes, yes, yes, let's go!"

Betsy grumbled, climbing into the back seat, "This is not a race, you know."

"Well, of course it isn't!" said Lars. "Otherwise we'd be lined up at a starting line so's everyone would leave at the same time. Which way out of town?"

"We're not going out of town, we're supposed to go someplace around here for lunch."

"Jill, we don't have time for lunch!"

Betsy said, "But I'm hungry."

Jill said, "Me, too. And anyway, it's included in the entry fee."

Jill was not a little woman, but Lars was very large, and when he turned toward her, his expression angry, he seemed very intimidating. But she had that special look of her own, one that simply absorbed his anger and frustration, giving nothing back and leaving him deflated. He sighed, "Oh, well, what the hell. Which way?"

"Go to the corner and turn right. Go one block and turn left on Sibley."

"Right," said Lars, settling himself in the driver's seat. He opened the throttle about a third of the way, and the Stanley obediently pulled smoothly away. Lars appeared resigned to lunch, but as they rounded the corner at the end of the block, the car let loose a loud and angry *Whooooo, whoo-whoo!*, making pedestrians jump and stare. Some waved, laughing at their own surprise. One exception was a young man standing in the dark, wet ruins of a two-liter bottle of Coke. His gesture was unkind.

Jill read instructions until they were safely parked at Peters on the Lake. " 'Please remember to order from the Antique Car menu,' " she concluded.

"Hey, Smith is here, too," said Lars, nodding at the long and beautiful Renault parked in a distant and shady corner.

"Wow," said Jill, pausing to stare.

"Come on," said Lars. "Let's order sandwiches to go."

"We will sit at a table and eat like civilized persons," said Jill.

Lars sighed, but said nothing, not even when Jill asked for soup and a salad.

They joined Adam Smith, who greeted Betsy warmly and shook hands with Lars and Jill. Betsy said, "Are you giving someone a ride back?"

Adam said, "No, but if you'd care to join me again, that would be great."

Jill gave Betsy an encouraging look, but Betsy said, "No, I think I'll stay with the Stanley." The fact that he was unafraid to answer more of her questions meant either that he had no guilty knowledge or was very confident of his answers.

In another few minutes more people joined them, and the talk became strictly about the cars. Betsy listened anyway, hoping to pick up something useful.

Mike Jimson grumped to Adam, "I took your advice and resleeved the number two cylinder. I thought the rod was rapping, but you were right, it was the piston slapping. The clearance was great. I don't know why it was doing that."

The man beside Mike was saying, "That damn foot brake locks. I use it and I got to stop and release it by hand, so I was taking my foot off the gas and yanking on the hand brake, and be dipped if it don't work like a charm, finished the run, and got my fourth medallion."

The woman beside him said, "I told Frank he ought to soak that Caddy in LokTite and see if that won't keep parts from falling off. Sometimes I think I spend half our time on the road stopping to run back and pick something up. Today it was the license plate and one of the bolts off a fender."

Adam told Jill, "It was Leland and Falkner got Henry Ford's second failure at car making to run, you know."

Betsy had taken only a few bites of her sandwich when Lars stood. "Come on," he said, dropping a heavy damask napkin on his empty plate, having inhaled the roast beef sandwich that ornamented it only minutes before. "See you in New London," he said to the table, a wicked glint in his eye.

"This isn't a race, Mr. Larson," said a woman, glinting back.

"No, it sure isn't," agreed Lars. "But I left the pilot light burning, so I should get back out there. Come on, you two."

Betsy brought the uneaten portion of her sandwich with her.

Jill got them out onto Meeker County 31, where there was a straight run of several miles, before turning to Betsy to ask something about Adam Smith. Betsy couldn't understand half the words, even though Jill was shouting. Once Lars got out on the highway, he had opened the throttle, and there was a mad tumble of wind over the upright windshield that tangled Jill's ash-blond hair and lifted Betsy's dress indecently.

Betsy, trying to eat her tuna fish sandwich with one hand and hold her dress down with the other, said, "I can't hear you," mouthing the words elaborately.

Jill turned to shout at Lars, "Slow down, for heaven's sake!"

"And let that lah-dee-dah French car pass me?" Lars replied, tightening his grip on the steering wheel.

So Jill sat down again. Betsy gave up on her sandwich to exalt in the smooth, fast run, and waved at the occasional car or pedestrian or bicyclist as the Steamer rushed past them.

Lars pulled into a gas station at the intersection with Tri-County Road. "We're just over twenty-one miles from Litchfield, so this is placed perfect for us to stop and take on water."

He steered over to the side of the building and this time ignored the instant crowd his car attracted. Jill got out so he could get out. "Have you got a water hose I can use?" he asked the man who came out of the station to stare.

Jill climbed into the back seat and said to Betsy, "Talk fast."

"Adam said Bill was angry with him over the car, but even angrier because Adam beat him in a race to be president of the Antique Car Club."

"What do you think?"

"Well, Adam didn't seem angry himself, but of course he wouldn't, he knows he's a suspect. And he hasn't got an alibi. What I don't like is that he was late getting to St. Paul, arriving way behind Mildred Feeney, who is very elderly and therefore hardly a speed demon."

"So you think he's the one?"

"I don't know. He said if Minnesota had the death penalty, he'd be living in Costa Rica right now."

"Let's go!" said Lars, and Jill got out to follow Lars back into the front seat. "Got the route sheet?" he asked, checking his gauges.

"Right here," said Jill. "We need to get an odometer on this thing. The directions keep telling us how many miles to turnoffs and I can't estimate mileage. And another thing, we made that twenty-one miles in something less than twenty minutes. The speed limit out here is fifty-five. If you don't drive slower, we're going to get a speeding ticket, and think how that poor schnook of a trooper is going to feel testifying how he wrote up a 1912 automobile?"

"He won't have to testify, I'll plead guilty!" said Lars proudly, and Jill sighed.

But he did slow down a bit. Still, they arrived at the American Legion building in New London well ahead of the others. The downstairs of the new-looking building was mostly a wide and low barroom, the decor heavily patriotic. It was well lit and deliciously cool. Betsy went to the rest room to find a comb and spend several minutes wrenching it through her hair. Those long veils women wore when riding in these cars seemed a lot less ridiculous now, especially considering that they wore their hair long. She went back out and ordered a Diet Coke at the bar.

It was fifteen minutes before Adam Smith came in, and forty minutes before the Winton's owner and his wife showed up. Adam smiled at Lars and greeted him, but said nothing about coming in second, nor did the Winton's owners say anything about finishing third. Then again, only the first-place driver had a mayonnaise stain on his shirt from hurtling through his lunch.

Betsy allowed Mike to buy her a refill and sat down at a little round table with a big bowl of pretzels on it to talk with him and Dorothy.

"I understand Bill Birmingham ran against Adam for the presidency of your club," she said after pleasantries had been exchanged.

Dorothy nodded, but said, "It was more like Adam ran against Bill, wasn't it, Mike?"

Mike said, "Sort of. Our outgoing president was moving to Arizona as soon as his term was up, and Bill, who was vice president, kind of thought the office was his by right. He was an effective VP, and since he'd cut back to half-time at his company, he had the time. Adam was route manager, you know, getting out maps and driving the back roads, laying out the runs. Important, but not management. And no one knew at the time he was about to retire, not even him, we think."

Dorothy put in, "Also right about then, their youngest went off to college and Adam's wife, who probably had been waiting for that to happen, divorced him. That was last fall, and he suddenly had all the time in the world to devote to his cars and the club."

"What did he do for a living?"

"Upper management," said Mike. "CEO, in fact. Only been there six or seven years."

Dorothy said with a significant eyebrow lift, "But they gave him one heck of a golden parachute, and he'd been given stock options in lieu of cash bonuses the whole time he'd been there, so he is simply *rolling* in it. So it doesn't matter that he can't find another job in his field." Again the eyebrow lifted and she nodded weightily.

Mike said, "He didn't do anything dishonest. From what I've heard, he had a theory of management that made him a lot of enemies. Plus the last company he was with . . . Well, it's going to take them a few years to get back on course." He looked at his wife. "He's like Bill was, in some respects. When he thinks he's right, he goes full out for it, and hang the consequences."

They talked awhile longer, then Betsy went back to Jill. The place had filled up with antique car owners, their spouses and even some children, other friends and passengers, and townsfolk wanting to meet the owners of those strange old cars. "Where's Lars?" asked Betsy, unable to spot him in the crowd.

"He's here, making the rounds, talking cars and engines and the run tomorrow."

"Jill, are you okay with this new interest of his?"

Jill sighed. "I guess so. The cars are beautiful, and the people who own them seem nice enough. And now that I'm more confident that Lars knows what he's doing with the Stanley, I enjoy riding around in it. On the other hand, this is a very expensive hobby he's gotten into. It's a comfort to know that while Lars can get very crazy about something, it never lasts forever."

"Except you?" asked Betsy with a smile.

"Okay, except me."

Lars circulated for a while, finished his third beer, and came back to ask Jill, "Are we staying here for dinner? They're setting up a big grill outside, and I hear their burgers are great."

Betsy said, "How about I take you and Jill to the Blue Heron in Willmar? It's supposed to be very nice. I left my copy of the *Excelsior Bay Times* at the motel, and it has a nice picture of you and your Steamer in it."

"Really? Well, sure, I wouldn't mind having a look at it. How about you, Jill?"

"Fine. We can't talk here, anyhow. How about we follow you in my car, Betsy, so you don't have to drive us back."

The Blue Heron was a Frank Lloyd Wright–style building on top of a hill overlooking Lake Willmar. It was the clubhouse of a private golf course, but the restaurant on the second floor was open to the public. The far wall and the long adjacent wall were made of panes of thermal glass and overlooked a putting green and the lake.

The hostess at first said there would be a wait, but when Betsy gave her name, she said, "Oh, there's someone from your party here already, holding a table for you."

Betsy followed her to a table by the longer wall, where Sergeant Morrie Steffans rose to his considerable height as they approached. He looked pleased, or perhaps amused, at her surprise.

"How did you know we'd be coming here?" asked Betsy as he came around to hold her chair for her.

"I'm a detective, remember?"

She frowned at him, so he elaborated. "One of your employees told me where you were staying. I drove out here and had a talk with the manager. He told me he always recommended the Blue Heron to those guests who like poached salmon and the Ramble Inn to those who like deep-fried perch. Somehow you struck me as a salmon person so, like the salmon, I swam upstream to here." He smiled at Betsy, who, rather to her surprise, found herself smiling back.

She introduced Jill and Lars, and he said, "What, you collect cops as a hobby?"

"No, Jill was my sister's best friend and I guess I sort of inherited her. Lars is Jill's steady. He's the reason we're here for the run. He owns a Stanley Steamer."

"Yes, I guessed that by the scorch marks," said Steffans.

Lars put the hand with the scald into his lap. "These things happen until you learn the tricks of the boiler," he said.

"There must be compensations, then," said Steffans and he listened with apparent interest while Lars rode his hobby horse for a while. When the waitress arrived with the menus, Steffans said, "I understand you do a beautiful poached salmon here."

"We do," she said, "but we had a big crowd at lunch and they all ordered it, so we're out until Sunday," and looked confused when this amused everyone at the table. "We have some very nice lamb chops," she offered and was reassured when this didn't set off another round of laughter.

Betsy and Steffans had the lamb, Lars ordered a porterhouse steak, and Jill decided to try the stuffed chicken breast, another specialty of the house. No one wanted a predinner drink, so the waitress went to fetch their salads.

•   •   •

Marvin and Charlotte watched Betsy go into the restaurant from the bar. "Who are those two with her?" asked Marvin.

"I don't know—wait, that man was driving the Stanley last Saturday, and Betsy told me she was sponsoring the Stanley. I don't remember his name. He's new to the Antique Car Club."

"So he's not a cop."

"I don't know what he does, she didn't say."

"Who's the other woman?"

"I don't know. But it doesn't matter. What matters is they didn't stay for the barbecue in New London, so we can talk to them about Adam without anyone else in the club seeing us and telling him about it."

They gave Betsy and her friends a few minutes, then strolled casually into the dining room. They were halfway across when they saw Betsy and then the fourth person at her table. "Oh, my God, it's that Minnetonka detective!" murmured Charlotte, gripping Marvin's arm to bring him to a halt. She would have turned around except the detective had already seen her. His look of surprise brought the attention of the others.

Betsy lifted a hand and said, "Well, hello, what are you doing here?"

Charlotte led Marvin to the table. "I was feeling caged," she said, "and I just wanted to go for a long drive. Marvin has a convertible, and the night was warm, and before we realized it, we were nearly to Willmar. Then I remembered this as a nice place, and we decided to stop in."

Steffans, with old-fashioned manners, had risen to his feet as Charlotte came to them, and after a puzzled moment, so did Lars. Betsy performed the introductions.

Charlotte said, a trifle dryly, "Yes, Sergeant Steffans and I have already met. And he's talked with Marvin Pierce, too." To Lars: "That's a beautiful Stanley you bought. I hope you have many happy miles in her." To Jill: "I think Betsy mentioned you to me. It's needlepoint you do? I'm a counted cross stitcher."

"Won't you join us?" said Steffans. "We just placed our order, but we can get the waitress back, I'm sure."

"No, no," said Marvin, beginning to turn away. "We don't want to interrupt your conversation."

Charlotte added, "Besides, there's no room."

But Steffans was already moving his chair to one side so he could bring the small table behind him up. "See how easy it is to fix that? Now, Mrs. Birmingham, you sit right here, and Marvin, you sit there, and I'll just go find our waitress." He gave a sort of bow, and was halfway across the room in a couple of long-legged strides.

Charlotte looked around the table with an uncomfortable smile. "Goodness, isn't he the managing kind? He must have been terrific at directing traffic!"

Betsy, laughing with the others, said, "I hope you don't mind. By the way, have you seen this week's *Excelsior Bay Times?* I brought it along because there's a a beautiful photograph of Lars with his Stanley. But there's a photograph of Bill, too, working on his Maxwell."

"There is?" said Charlotte. "Well, isn't that interesting. I remember you saying there was a reporter in Excelsior covering the run, but I didn't see him. May I see it?"

Betsy handed it across to her. "It's in the middle, lots of pictures."

Charlotte opened the paper and ran her eyes quickly over the photographs. She gave a little scream when she saw the Maxwell with a white flannel rump hiding most of the hood and engine. "Oh, my God, Bill would have hated to see that!" she said, and handed it to Marvin. "Isn't that just awful?" she said, and laughed. But she felt her lips twist and her eyes began to sting. "Excuse me, I'm sorry," she said and fished in her purse for a handkerchief. "I had to dig this old thing out," she said, waving it in her hand before dabbing her eyes. "My mother always carried one, but I never did until this happened to Bill. The oddest things set me off crying, and I just hate those wads of Kleenex." She touched her nose but didn't blow it. "I'm sorry," she said again.

"We understand," said Jill.

Marvin, shaking his head, said, "It's a shame this had to be the last picture taken of Bill. Not exactly his best side."

"Oh, stop it, Marvin!" said Charlotte, trying not to laugh, and dabbing at more tears.

Marvin said to Betsy, "Charlotte told me you investigate crimes, is that true?"

Betsy nodded. "Yes, as an amateur. I seem to have a knack for it."

"I also hear you're looking into Bill's death. What have you found out?"

"A number of things. Broward, for example, was unhappy with his father's continuing interference in Birmingham Metal Fabrication, as you undoubtedly know."

Charlotte felt a cold hand grip her heart. "You can't possibly think my son would murder his own father!"

she said in a quiet voice she hardly recognized as her own.

Betsy's look did nothing to warm the grip. "I'm sorry, but I do," she said. "Unless you can think of a better candidate?"

Charlotte exchanged a look with Marvin. "Well, as a matter of fact, I can. We can, Marvin and I."

16

Detective Sergeant Morrie Steffans, one of those people who pays attention, didn't have to ask who the waitress was for his table. He quickly picked her out from the quartet serving the room, and went to waylay her on her way from another table to tell her there were two new people at Betsy Devonshire's.

But he didn't go immediately back to his table. He stood a minute or two, watching Charlotte Birmingham and Marvin Pierce talking to Betsy, Jill, and Lars.

Lars, he knew, was an excellent patrol cop, very happy at his work, and therefore likely to stay on patrol until his back or his legs gave out. Which might be never—he looked built on the lines of the Stanley boiler he admired so much.

Jill, on the other hand, was on a different track. She had the quiet tenacity and wholesome integrity that would probably put her in a command position some-day. She might even wind up Chief of Police.

And then there was Ms. Devonshire. Wholly amateur, not at all disciplined or even learned in the field of investigation. Yet she'd broken several cases, most of them locally. She claimed, according to Sergeant Mike Malloy of the Excelsior Police Department, to be merely lucky, a sentiment he heartily endorsed. But luck was a genuine gift, a wonderful thing to be blessed with. Really legendary investigators had it, held on to it with both hands, and were deeply grateful for it. Malloy disliked Betsy, said she was an interfering civilian of the worst sort, by which he meant she was better than he was at solving crimes—at least the sort of crimes ordinary people got mixed up in, not the sort done by professional criminals. The ordinary crook could probably run rings around Ms. Devonshire, just as the pair at the table right now could run rings around Mike Malloy.

Steffans's eyes narrowed as he watched them work Betsy over. He didn't think for a minute they were fooling her. He began to walk slowly back to the table, his stuck-out ears already picking up the threads of the conversation.

Charlotte was here to protect her son Broward. To do that, she would see anyone else, *anyone*, indicted, convicted, and sentenced to life in prison. The best candidate she could find was Adam Smith, so here she was—and she didn't care if her story about just driving around aimlessly and just happening to stop at the Blue Heron was a little thin. It hadn't been hard to find Betsy Devonshire. A few phone calls and here she was. Sergeant

Steffans thought he was clever finding Betsy, but here was Charlotte, just as clever.

But Betsy's face showed only keen interest. "What have you found out about Adam Smith?" she asked.

Clever Charlotte let Marvin help dig the hole into which she hoped to push Adam.

Marvin said, "It's about the rivalry between Adam and Bill. I'm sure you know Bill bought a 1910 Fuller that Adam wanted, and wouldn't sell it to him. But that was only one round of an ongoing fight. Adam had previously bought a 1910 Maxwell that Bill wanted, even though Adam collects only rarities and Maxwells are about the most common pioneers around."

Jill said, "I thought you weren't an antique car owner, Marvin."

He said, surprised, "I'm not."

"But you know a lot about them."

He shrugged. "Heck, I've been friends with the Birminghams for a lot of years. You can't help picking up the language."

The police investigator's chair suddenly moved, and Sergeant Steffans sat down. "The waitress will be here in a minute," he said.

Charlotte said, "We were talking about how Adam Smith did things that showed he hated Bill. I think the worst was when Adam decided to run against Bill for president of the Minnesota Antique Car Club. Adam is route manager, that's what he does best, and he's always liked laying out the runs. Then Wesley Sweet decided to retire to Arizona. He was president for the past four terms. Bill was vice president for two, and he was very efficient, he did a lot of good work, so naturally he decided he had the best chance to be president. And like from out of left field"—Charlotte made a sharp gesture—"here comes Adam, hot to be president himself. And he runs the dirtiest, the hardest, the nastiest—"

"Now, Char, you're getting excited," interrupted Marvin quietly.

Charlotte's breath caught in her throat, but she stopped herself from saying something rude to Marvin. Because he was probably right, she had gotten carried away before. "Do you think so?" she said instead, making her voice sweetly humble. Marvin's smile of admiration made the sweetness genuine. "Well, maybe I am a little excited. But"—she turned her focus onto Betsy—"it was a very ugly campaign. Adam told lies about Bill, said he was incompetent, uncooperative, high-handed. It was just terrible, the things he said. I told Bill not to reply in kind, and I think that was a mistake, because Adam won by a very clear margin."

"But then why, if Adam won, would he murder Bill?"

"Oh, I'm not saying Adam murdered Bill because of the election. That would be ridiculous. I'm just telling you about it to show how deep the animosity went, that Adam really hated Bill."

"Because of the car thing," guessed Lars.

"No, the car thing was just another symptom. You know Adam was forced out of his position as CEO of General Steel?"

Betsy said, "I know he was given a golden parachute when he was asked to retire. I didn't know it was from General Steel."

"Well, Adam's method of improving a bottom line was to diversify. He was among the first practitioners of that. He wanted General Steel to get into manufacturing steel products as well as mining and smelting. He'd been expanding into a rolling mill already."

Steffans nodded. "I remember reading about that. The mill's in Gary, Indiana, I believe." He said to Betsy, who was giving him a surprised look, "One of my mutual funds is into metals."

Charlotte said, "Yes, well, a lot of the processing of taconite is done overseas nowadays, because it's cheaper. But instead of expanding into overseas processing, Adam decided to broaden his base, and he started looking at Birmingham Metal Fabrication." Charlotte smacked a hand onto the table to underline the enlightenment she saw in Betsy's eyes. "That's right, that's why Bill brought Broward into the company, to fight off Adam's attempt to buy us out. I was never so proud of both of them, the way they worked together to keep the company ours."

Lars said, frowning, "You mean General Steel wanted to do a hostile takeover?"

"No," said Charlotte, "you can only do a hostile takeover by buying up the stock of a publicly held company. We are family-owned. But Adam saw a clean, profitable, well-run company, and he started making offers."

"All you had to do was just say no, surely," said Betsy.

"You'd think so, wouldn't you? But Adam sent men in to talk to our employees, about a rival company that had better benefits, and hinting we were in financial trouble—lies, just like the lies he told about Bill during the election. That's how he works, not by showing he's better, but that the alternative is worse, getting everyone stirred up. Production was falling off and some of the men threatened to quit."

"So what did Bill and Broward do?" asked Lars.

"They sicced a lawyer on Adam's company. I don't know what the lawyer said, but a few months later Adam was out on his keester, and General Steel never bothered us again. They won't tell you so, of course, they have strict rules about privacy. But that's what happened." She saw belief on their faces and smiled.

The waitress took Charlotte and Marvin's order. Betsy made sure the waitress understood that she, Lars, and Jill were on one ticket.

The food, when it came, was delicious. Charlotte became intelligent and witty. Marvin, while more low key, was charming and funny. Betsy could see why Lisa Birmingham hoped one day the two would pair off.

It was Steffans who most surprised Betsy. He was relaxed, intelligent on a number of issues, nice without the least bit of condescension.

Toward the end of the meal, Charlotte asked Steffans point-blank, "Are you close to arresting someone for the murder of my husband?"

To Betsy's surprise, Steffans nodded. "As a matter of fact, I am. If I can get a few more answers, I might make an arrest tomorrow."

"Here at the run?" she asked, her attention almost painful in its intensity.

"Yes," he replied, and she relaxed all over. Betsy nodded to herself. *Broward's not coming to the run.* She thought, *Charlotte's glad he's safe.*

"But you're out of your jurisdiction," said Jill, faintly scandalized.

"Oh, I've been in touch with the Meeker County Sheriff, and I can get a warrant like that," he said, snapping his fingers.

"If you need backup, I'll be there tomorrow," said Lars.

"Me, too," said Jill, and there was a subtle shift in them, the way they sat, that linked them in a new way to Steffans. Betsy suddenly felt like an outsider.

"If you're handy, sure," said Steffans. Seeing the amazed look on Charlotte's face, he said, "I see you weren't properly introduced. These are Officers Jill Cross and Lars Larson, Excelsior PD."

Charlotte said angrily to Betsy, "You didn't tell me!"

Betsy replied mildly, "I didn't think it mattered. They aren't here in their official capacity, or at least they weren't until just now. Lars came as owner and driver of a car I'm sponsoring, and Jill really is his girl and my best friend."

"We understand," said Marvin, placatingly, speaking as much to Charlotte as to Betsy. "We're just a little surprised—which is understandable, considering the circumstances."

"And it's all right," said Steffans. "We're all still friends, right?"

"Right," agreed Marvin.

But it was a moment before Charlotte nodded agreement.

Still, the convivial mood was gone and the party began to break up. Soon Betsy found herself down in the small parking lot in front of the building, waving as Jill and Lars in one car, Charlotte and Marvin in another, pulled out and away.

Steffans stood beside Betsy until the cars' taillights disappeared around a bend.

Betsy asked, "Are you really going to arrest Adam Smith tomorrow?"

"No."

"Why did you say you would?"

"I said I might make an arrest tomorrow. But not Mr. Smith. He has an iron-clad alibi."

"Then who? Broward isn't here—is he?"

"Not as far as I know."

Charlotte had an iron-clad alibi of her own. *"Marvin?"*

"Come on, Ms. Devonshire. You've been dancing around the truth all evening. I could see it in your eyes. Let's go someplace and talk. Do you still have that copy of the *Excelsior Bay Times* with you? I want you to show me what you saw that none of the others did."

Saturday dawned cool and cloudy. Drivers listened to weather reports and studied the sky. Putting up the tops on the old cars that had them was a lengthy, difficult chore. They didn't like their bars being fitted into their slots, resisted having their braces tightened, and at every opportunity pinched blood blisters on fingers. Once they were up, they blocked vision, the wind roared under them loud enough to deafen a driver to other road hazards and they caught enough wind to slow travel. The only thing worse than struggling to put the top up before starting was stopping alongside the road in the rain to do it.

Most caved in and put tops up, swearing and complaining. The few who didn't claimed that since most did, it now certainly wasn't going to rain. "It's the opposite of washing your car," one said.

Lars shrugged off Betsy's suggestion that he put his top up. "I'm gonna go so fast I'll run between any raindrops," he boasted, then went back to recheck against his directions his list of places where water could be obtained, making sure he hadn't made a slip somewhere. Running his boiler dry would damage the hundreds of copper tubes inside it, a very expensive error.

Because the steamer was so fast, it was put near the back of the pack that gathered in a large church's parking lot the other side of the cemetery. Despite the threat of rain, a large crowd gathered to watch the old cars set off on their hundred-mile-plus run. Five church ladies had set up a table near the church hall's entrance, from which they dispensed cookies and coffee: free to drivers, a dollar a hit for onlookers. Beside the table was the car-run quilt, on its stand. Mildred Feeney, in a big flowered hat at least as old as she was, worked the crowd, selling last-chance raffle tickets. Two men from the American Legion, in uniform and with rifles, guarded the starting line, which had a tiny red-striped building beside it meant to look like a Cold Stream Guard's shelter. The mayor of New Brighton was on hand, in top hat and tails. *Talk about mixed messages,* thought Betsy, standing on the other side of the line from the mayor and the Cold Stream Guard shelter, clipboard in hand. She was herself wearing slacks, a blue-checked shirt, and sneakers—yet another fashion statement.

Off at the back of the parking lot a group of men with walkie-talkies and cell phones consulted under a big ham radio antenna. The leader of the pack was a

heavyset man leaning on a huge four-wheel-drive vehicle. Not police officers, these were the crew charged
with finding and rescuing old cars that faltered on the
journey.

The mayor, red-faced and sweating—his suit was
made of heavy wool, and it wasn't *that* cool—made a
brief speech honoring the people who found and restored these venerable ancestors of road travel. He said
he'd be on hand again in New Brighton to greet in
person every driver who completed the journey. He held
up a dull gold medallion the size of his palm and said
this was what the run was about, this was the prize to
be given to every car that finished the run. "Good luck
and God speed!" he concluded.

He stepped back and a man with a big green flag
came out from behind the guard shelter. The two American Legion veterans crossed to Betsy's side of the starting line, and Betsy checked the time on the big old
pocket watch Adam Smith had fastened to the top of
her clipboard. She looked at the 1902 Oldsmobile standing in quivering eagerness behind the line painted on
the blacktop. The man twirled his flag, and on dropping
it, the Legionnaires fired their rifles. The Oldsmobile
tottered across the line and rolled past the crowd cheer-
ing him on. Betsy put a checkmark next to the Oldsmobile's banner number and wrote the time down:
7:12 A.M.

By 8:30, most of the veterans had departed, and so
had perhaps half the crowd. Some were headed for Buffalo to watch the cars arrive for lunch, while others had
seen what they came to see and were headed somewhere else. Betsy could see Charlotte and Marvin now,
making their way closer to the starting line, looking for

Sergeant Steffans—who was closing in from behind.
They did, however, see the deputy sheriff off to their
right, moving toward them. Assuming he was heading
off Adam Smith, they altered course, toward the starting
line.

There was a roar of big engines as the follow-up
trucks started up, preparing to follow the line of antique
cars.

Betsy looked down the short line of cars still waiting
to begin their run. Lars was at the very end, behind
Adam in his Renault.

Charlotte and Marvin came close to the guard shelter
to watch two deputies and Jill approach as a 1908 Buick
in a bright shade of orange came up to the starting line.
A fast *pipe-pipe-pipe* started coming from the car, but
it slowed in tempo as the driver came to a stop, waiting
for the green flag. The piping was obviously connected
to the motor somehow, and by the grin of the driver,
something intentional. The flag dropped and the car
scuttled past the spectators, who made up in noise what
they lacked in numbers. The piping, which had in-
creased to a warble as he raced his engine, cut off as
he turned out of the parking lot onto the street.

Next was the 1912 Winton, a woman behind the
wheel wearing a pinch-brim cap turned rakishly backward and her male passenger, in shirtsleeves, waving
grandly; then the 1911 Marmon, whose driver sounded
its *ooooooo-gah!* over and over as he raced out of the
lot. Betsy noted the time of each, then turned to watch
Adam pull up in his huge and beautiful Renault touring
sports car. *He should have someone wearing Erte clothing in the backseat, perhaps with an Afghan hound,*
thought Betsy, smiling at him. While she would never

give up the right to wear trousers, a car like Adam's called for old-fashioned elegance.

The deputy stepped out into the starting lane behind the Renault.

Adam waved to the flagman, who raised his flag. The flag fell and the Renault pulled away and was gone, to the astonishment of Charlotte and Marvin.

Steffans, now immediately behind them, said something, and it was Charlotte who realized first what was about to happen—and she helped Marvin get away. She raised a bloodcurdling scream and flew into Steffans, knocking him down. She fell on him, clawing and scratching and still screaming. People behind them hastily backed away.

Marvin hot-footed it across the starting line, brushing past Betsy—who was stupidly frozen to the spot—to the huge four-wheel-drive SUV, where he did a very credible stiff-arm block on the heavyset man who tried to get in his way.

The heavyset man fell, Marvin jumped in the vehicle, and the man did a spectacular leap from the ground, much like a freshly landed fish, landing out of the way as the SUV bolted forward.

Betsy found her voice and yelled, "Stop him!" as Marvin roared out of the lot.

One of the deputies trying to untangle Steffans and Charlotte looked up and raced off, bound for his patrol car at the far end of the lot.

Jill stepped in to grab Charlotte by the hair with one hand and her arm with another. "That's enough!" she said.

Betsy ran to the Stanley, wrenched open the door,

and said, "Let's go!" (Though she later remembered it as, "Follow that car!")

Lars shoved the throttle all the way open, the steamer's tires screamed, and Betsy was flung back into her seat. By the time she got herself untangled, the Stanley was flying up the street, actually gaining on the SUV. Lars grabbed a brass-headed knob and the Stanley's whistle gave a long blast, causing innocent cars to swerve out of their way.

Marvin slewed crazily making the turn onto the highway, but the SUV was surefooted enough to cling to the road. Marvin got back into the right lane and floored it, and the big gas engine responded with a will.

So he must have been horrified a few seconds later to look in his rearview mirror and see an antique car still gaining on him.

Betsy, hanging on to the gas lever, was yelling encouragement at Lars, who had a fierce grin on his face.

But as they closed the gap, Betsy began to worry. How would they make Marvin stop? Was Lars going to try to pass him and cut him off? What if Marvin just crashed into them? Suddenly the Stanley's rooflessness, its lack of seat belts, made it a very dangerous place to be.

The SUV's brake lights came on, and the gap closed swiftly.

"He's giving up!" said Betsy, vastly relieved. Lars shut down his throttle, and Betsy remembered how weak the primitive brakes were. They were going to overshoot. Lars would have to stop down the road and turn around. No cars oncoming, good. She looked behind. No flashing lights and sirens, just a single private car, well back.

But Marvin wasn't finished yet. There was a grassy lane across the broad ditch that ran alongside the highway, an access lane for a farmer to get into his field. The SUV swerved onto it and crashed through the pipe-and-wire gate into the pasture. Grazing cows, startled, began to move.

Lars braked, but the Stanley was already past the lane.

"Hang on!" yelled Lars and the Stanley bounced off the highway, *down* into the wide ditch, and t-W-i-S-t-e-D its way up out of the ditch. Chuffing under the load, it nevertheless went through the barbed wire fence as if it wasn't there.

The SUV was ahead of them, climbing a steepish slope, bouncing and skidding, flinging sod, mud and worse in all directions. Cows, only as alarmed as calm and stupid animals can get, scattered slowly.

The Stanley might have been on a country road, climbing the hill smoothly and effortlessly.

On the other side of the slope were the remains of a woodlot: stumps and fallen logs, heaps of brush, mudholes. The SUV swerved and slid between the obstacles, bottoming here and there. A hubcap flew off. Marvin tried to dodge back toward the highway and snagged his exhaust on a stump. It tore loose and suddenly his engine was very loud.

The Stanley went over everything. This was common terrain when it was on the design board, and its big wheels kept the underside clear of obstructions. Lars, after years of hard driving, with special law-enforcement training and the amazing Stanley to ride, kept thwarting Marvin and his SUV's every attempt to regain the highway.

Betsy, hanging on like grim death, watched the SUV finally dodge wildly around the last heap of brush, then crush another barbed wire fence. They were still on downhill terrain, and the SUV gained speed as it roared into a field that some hopeful farmer had plowed, harrowed, and planted with corn that had sprouted into neat rows of green about eight inches high. "Got 'im now!" Lars crowed, though Betsy couldn't see how.

The SUV destroyed the sprouting plants in their hundreds as it veered down the gray-black field. It started up another slope, this one steeper than the last, slowing as it went, fishtailing madly, earth and small green plants flying in all directions. The big whip aerial on the back was flailing as if wielded by a mad driver and the horses under the hood were real and needed beating to greater effort.

Lars was by now close enough that some clods struck his windshield. By the time they reached the top, the SUV, despite its roaring engine and whipping aerial, was barely making any progress at all—and blocking its passage was a white board fence. On the other side, a dozen flesh and blood horses stood, heads raised in amazement.

The SUV lacked momentum to break this fence down. By twisting the wheel hard, Marvin managed to turn and start along it, Lars close behind.

"He's going to get away, isn't he?" said Betsy, as the SUV started again to build speed.

"Nah, there's another fence up ahead. I'll corner him there."

And he did. Marvin tried to turn, but Lars was crowding him in his outer rear quarter, and Marvin ended up hard against the fence, too close to open his door. Lars shut the throttle down and leaped out of his car all in one movement. Before Betsy could even think what to do, Lars was sprawled across the hood of the SUV, pointing a gun at Marvin through the windshield, yelling at him to shut the engine off.

Marvin shut the engine off and raised his hands.

Lars called, "Betsy, blow the whistle until you see some backup coming."

Betsy pulled the brass-headed knob on the dash, sending the horses in the meadow into wild flight. She blew a long and then a row of shorts, then a long again. She kept doing it.

It seemed like a long time before a farmer drove up on an immense tractor, curious to know what these people were doing in his field. He had a cell phone in a pocket.

"So it was Marvin after all?" said Godwin from a stool in the corner. He was wearing immaculate white shoes, socks, and trousers, and not anxious to get anything greasy on them. His pearl-gray silk shirt was also vulnerable and he hitched the stool just a little bit farther from the wall where, he was sure, spiders lurked. Godwin was not afraid of spiders, but surely their little feet were dirty from crawling up and down that dusty wall. If one got on him, it might leave a *trail*. He had a date with John for dinner, and John had sounded very quiet and gentle when he'd called yesterday. Things were going to be all right, probably, but Godwin always felt more confident when he was dressed especially well.

"No, it was both of them," said Betsy.

She was sitting on a low rolling chest designed to be sat upon, made of plastic, used by gardeners who didn't like stooping or kneeling but who had a long row to plant or weed. She was wearing denim shorts and a sleeveless pink blouse, although she was getting too old to be going sleeveless, except among friends.

But everyone present was a friend. Jill was there, sitting on the workbench, her bruises from the fight with Charlotte making bold purple comments on her smooth complexion.

And Lars, of course, since this was his barn. He was in his grubbiest jeans and T-shirt, under the Stanley, "swaging the boiler"—banging a shaped metal plug up the numberless copper tubes, making them round again. It was a long, long job. He'd divided the tubes into areas, and worked on one area at a time; otherwise, he'd fall into despair at the large number there were to swage.

During the wait for backup to arrive, the boiler had run itself dry. Lars should have told Betsy to shut it down, close off the valves, but he'd been concentrating on keeping Marvin from doing something stupid.

Betsy took most of the blame. She should have thought of it, paid attention to the gauges. But the Stanley had sat there in silence and she had fallen into her internal combustion habit of thinking a silent car was a car shut off, and so the boiler was scorched.

"How do you know it was both of them?" asked Godwin.

"Because that was the only way everything fit. She was the one who pulled the trigger. She shot him early in the morning of the Excelsior run, as they were getting ready to leave the house for St. Paul. Then she called Marvin, and he came over and took Bill's body over to the lay-by in the trunk of his car. Charlotte followed with the trailer they hauled the Maxwell in. It was Marvin who drove the Maxwell in the run, not Bill."

"But surely people talked to Bill," objected Godwin. "How could they mistake Marvin for him?"

"Actually they didn't really talk to him. Charlotte stayed with Marvin until he was parked. She talked to Adam and to anyone who came by, until Marvin was well under the hood and able just to grunt at anyone who tried to talk to him."

"Why would Marvin help her like that?" asked Godwin.

"Because they were lovers, had been for years. Everything was okay until Bill started spending more time at home. Then he got suspicious. Marvin wanted Charlotte to divorce Bill, but Marvin wasn't a wealthy man. And while Bill wasn't taking care of his high blood pressure, he may have had his suspicions about Marvin confirmed before he had that fatal stroke everyone was anticipating."

"Golden handcuffs," said Godwin sadly.

"Yes, at least in part. But also, tyrants don't make loving husbands."

"What do you think, she just decided she'd had enough and shot him?" asked Jill.

"I don't think so. She's a very intelligent person, she would have had a better plan set up in advance. I think she told the truth in her confession; they had a quarrel, he got violent, which he'd done before, and she went for the gun and shot him."

"Self-defense, then?" asked Godwin.

"Detective Steffans says no. She had to go into another room, unlock a drawer, and then go back with it. She could have left the house instead. On the other hand, one reason she wore those enveloping dresses was because sometimes she had to hide bruises. Bill struck her often, but was careful to hit her in places she could cover up with clothing."

"The monster!" said Godwin, with a shiver.

"So what put you on to them?" asked Jill.

"Orts," said Betsy.

That had been said into a break in the hammering from Lars, and he wheeled himself out from under his car long enough to inquire, "Orts?"

"Those little pieces of floss you cut off the end of a row of stitching. When you run it down so short you can't take another stitch. The end you cut off is an ort."

"Oh," he said and went back to hammering.

"What about orts?" persisted Jill.

"The photographs of the crime scene you brought me, remember? There were orts on Bill's trousers, just like they were on Charlotte's dress. She said she left them wherever she stitched. Anyone who lay on the floor of her sewing room—where the shooting took place— would come away with orts all over his clothes. But the man who drove into Excelsior and dove under the hood of his car to repair it, had no orts on his trousers. That photograph of him in the *Excelsior Bay Times* showed them immaculately clean, as clean as Godwin over there."

Godwin looked down at himself, then smiled at Betsy. "Thank you," he said.

"That's it?" said Jill. "Just because of some orts?"

"Well, there were some other things. The way she knew what Marvin was thinking when they came into my shop without his saying a word was exactly the way she knew what 'Bill' was thinking when he was sitting beside her in the Maxwell. I thought she did that with everyone she knew well, but she didn't do it with anyone else. The smile she gave Marvin at the Courage Center pool was the same she gave the person we all thought was her husband. When I found out what kind of a tyrant Bill was, I wondered how Charlotte could feel so affectionate toward him. The answer was, she couldn't."

Godwin said, "So you just put it all together in your usual clever way."

Betsy frowned. "I tried to think of other explanations, but none worked. Broward acted badly about my investigating because he thought he was the only one who knew about Marvin and Charlotte's affair and was trying to prevent my finding out and telling his sister and brothers. Charlotte lied when she said Bro and Bill teamed up to keep Adam from taking Birmingham Metal."

"How'd you find that out?" asked Jill.

"I didn't. Steffans did. Bro told him the reason he came home was because he heard from Bill's doctor that if Bill didn't retire, he'd be dead in six months. Since Bro knew Steffans was looking for motives, Bro had every reason to point at Adam—and he did tell him about the Fuller and the race for president of the car club.

"And there was an accident in the tunnel that Saturday, just as Adam said, so his alibi checked out. So it wasn't Broward and it wasn't Adam."

She turned to Jill. "Another thing that bothered me was the medical examiner's statement about time of death." She turned to Jill. "You know what I mean. The estimate was, he died between late Friday night and

noon on Saturday. That makes the window curiously
lopsided, if he'd been killed in that lay-by around noon.
But if he was killed early in the morning, that was right
in the middle of the window."

Jill nodded. "I see what you mean."

"I thought for a long while it was Marvin who did
the whole thing, shot Bill and hid his body in the lay-
by. But when? The night before? Marvin had an alibi
for the night before; he was playing poker with some
friends. Maybe late at night, after the poker game, or
the day of the run, early in the morning. I thought about
Bill going to confront Marvin over the affair he was
having with Charlotte. I thought perhaps Marvin shot
him when Bill got violent, and then, to cover the time
of the murder, he took Bill's place, driving the Maxwell
in the run. But why bring Charlotte into it? He could
just bury the body somewhere, or make it look like a
robbery. Surely Marvin would never ask the woman he
loved to be an accessory to murder. But if Marvin drove
the Maxwell, Charlotte *was* right in the middle of the
cover-up, deeply involved.

"So I thought she must be the one who shot him—
only not at the lay-by, she was with me all day Saturday. Then I thought, well, what if she shot him early
Saturday morning, when they were getting ready for the
run? Then, okay, it still was Marvin doing the driving.
She called Marvin to help her, and they came up with
this hasty scheme. And there it was, all the pieces in
place."

"Clever of her to get you to provide her with an alibi," said Godwin.

"No, it wasn't," said Jill. "She didn't know about
Betsy's sleuthing skills or she would never have in-

volved her. Once she found out Betsy has a nose for crime, she had to pretend she wanted Betsy to investigate, which was really the last thing on earth she wanted."

Betsy nodded. "And because she was scared of what I might find out, she kept coming around to check on me. That was another thing that made me look at her. She couldn't wait for me to come to her, she just had to find out if I was getting close. When she turned up in Willmar to shove Adam under my nose, I knew I was right."

"That's two police investigators you've gotten in ahead of," said Godwin. "Sergeant Mike Malloy and now Detective Steffans."

But Betsy shook her head. "No, he was onto her as well. He followed her out to Willmar because he was afraid she might try to murder me. While she was out there, he had a forensics team picking up all kinds of evidence in her house."

Godwin cocked his head at her. "You like him, don't you?"

"Heavens no!" said Betsy. "For one thing, he's too tall and gawky. For another, his ears stick out. For another . . ." She tried to think of a personality trait to complain about, but once she started thinking about his shy smile, his charming wit, the way he looked at her with admiring eyes, she had to stop, because she couldn't think of anything else. ✳

Fabric: Aida, White, or Black
Design Count: 73w x 79h
Design Size: 7.3 x 7.9 in, 10 Count

Key: • DMC 928 Grey Green-VY LT
      ☐ DMC 931 Antique Blue-MD
      ◉ DMC 932 Antique Blue-LT
      ✖ DMC 3727 Antique Mauve-LT
      ■ DMC 3787 Brown Grey-DK

The designer, Denise E. Williams, stitched this design on black 14-count Aida. On any other color fabric, stitch the design first, and then fill in the blank stitch spaces using DMC Black.

Hints

1. Take the pattern to a copy shop and enlarge it so the markings in the squares are easy to read.

2. Find and mark the center of the pattern, and the center of your fabric.

3. If you use black fabric, put a white cloth behind it to make the weave easier to see.

4. This pattern is trickier than it looks. Count twice so you only have to stitch once.

Coming October 2004

❊❊❊❊❊

Crewel Yule

A new needlework mystery by

Monica Ferris

❊❊❊❊❊

Snow is not the only thing falling in
Nashville this December. The yuletide cheer
of the needlework market at the
Consulate Hotel is tragically disturbed when
Belle Hammermill, a Milwaukee shop owner,
tumbles nine stories to her death.

Betsy Devonshire is the only witness to the
fall, and it's up to her to determine if her
fellow needleworkers have Christmas—
or murder—on their minds.

0-425-19827-8

❊❊❊❊❊

A Berkley Prime Crime Hardcover